PORTERHOUSE

GRADE-A BEEFCAKES SERIES - BOOK 4

VANESSA VALE

Porterhouse

Cover design: Bridger Media

Cover graphic: Deposit Photos: area; Period Images

GET A FREE BOOK!

JOIN MY MAILING LIST TO BE THE
FIRST TO KNOW OF NEW RELEASES,
FREE BOOKS, SPECIAL PRICES AND
OTHER AUTHOR GIVEAWAYS.

http://freeromanceread.com

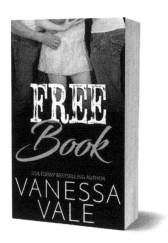

Women. The saying went, can't live with them, can't live without them. I would agree to that, except it wasn't all women. Just one in particular. Jill Murphy. I couldn't live with her because she wasn't ready yet to do more than date casually. The fact that she wanted me *and* Liam Hogan but hadn't let herself admit that yet was probably the reason. We weren't helping her with that all too much since she didn't know we were both totally on board with it. He and I had met and agreed we'd claim her together. Why fight when we could both have her? Two men taking care of her, loving her, protecting her was better for Jill. She'd always have a man to lean on, to take care of her every need.

We both wanted her. Both ached for her. Both needed inside her, and soon. I could sway a jury in the courtroom with strategic words and a solid argument. But Jill wasn't a case to win, but a heart to covet. It was important she came to the decision that she belonged to both of us on her own. We wanted her all-in, heart and soul. And luscious body.

So no living with her. Yet.

As for living without her? Not happening. No fucking

way. Just seeing her face light up when she saw me made my day. My week. Hell, my entire fucking life.

Jillian Murphy was mine. All mine, and Liam's too. We'd live with her, claim her, keep her, cherish the fuck out of her and never spend a night without her beside one of us.

But first, she had to agree.

Women.

I COULD HEAR my cell ringing from the depths of my purse, but I wasn't taking my hands off the steering wheel to search for it, no matter how eager I was to answer. Not with the snow on the road. The latest few inches were fresh and the plows had been through, but they didn't use salt or scrape all the way down to the pavement, so the streets of Raines were a hard crust of white until the spring thaw. And that wasn't for a few more months.

A spot on the street was easy to find, and I pulled in and shut off the engine. I'd been in newer models that allowed a cell phone to sync into the dashboard for hands free calling, but that wasn't something available in my older model SUV. It ran, had heat—which was great since it was close to zero—and it was mine free and clear.

I dug through my purse, found the cell. I thought it might be Porter telling me he was running late because he was coming from work in Clayton, but it was Parker Drew instead.

"You're going to talk to them, right?" she asked, not bothering with a warm up 'hello'. "No chickening out."

I rolled my eyes. "Yes. Tonight's the night."

"You sound a little panicked."

"I *am* a little panicked," I admitted. "I mean, why shouldn't I be? It's not that often a guy gets told he's not enough, and that a woman wants him *and* his best friend."

"Neither of them is going to think that," she countered.

The butterflies in my stomach were telling me otherwise. "I hope not, but it's a possibility I could end up with neither of them."

"Porter's a Duke and having two guys claim one woman is a Duke thing. I mean, look at me."

"You've got three," I corrected. She was dating—a very bland term for what she had going—Porter's cousin, Gus Duke, as well as two other guys, Kemp and Poe.

"You've been up front with them all along that you were interested in both of them. It's not like anyone can get away with dating two men at the same time on the sly in a town the size of Raines without them hearing about it."

I was dating Porter Duke *and* Liam Hogan, the new sheriff of Raines County. Right from the start, I'd told them I wanted to keep things casual. Not exclusive. Well, I was exclusively dating the two of them, but not together. I'd been interested in being with both of them all along, together, but had no idea how to tell them that. I still didn't, but tonight I was doing it anyway.

I *really* liked them. No, I'd fallen. Hard. Not just for Porter or Liam, but for Porter *and* Liam.

"I work too much to do anything but take it slow," I told her. I was a nurse and worked full-time at the hospital. Three twelve-hour shifts in the recovery room at the beginning of the week, then I co-shared a job at a doctor's office with a woman who'd just had a baby and wanted to cut back to part-time. It worked for both of us to split the full-time position, so I worked there Thursdays and Fridays. Dr. Metzger was a sweetheart and had talked to me about continuing my nursing education, but that wasn't going to happen. I didn't have time for that, not much free time for anything beyond sleeping in, doing laundry and errands. Especially not tons of time for a boyfriend... or two.

I had the hots for Porter and Liam—to put the feelings I had mildly—and I'd wanted to get to know both of them. They'd been receptive to fun, easy dates and the fact that I was going out with the other. Over the past few months, we'd gone, separately, to dinner, hiking, even bowling. Both were charming, smart, successful men—sexy, too—and I wanted both. Everything we did only confirmed that. Parker and her men proved that I could have both Porter and Liam, that my heart didn't have to settle. And she wasn't the only one. Ava, who ran the Seed and Feed, was engaged to Colton Ridge and Tucker Duke, another one of Porter's cousins. *Two men.*

"Honey, glaciers move faster than you do," Parker added.

I frowned at her words, although she couldn't see me. We'd been friends growing up, but had lost touch over the years. She'd moved back to town a few months ago to be the temporary sheriff and we'd reconnected. The fact that she'd been Liam's boss for a few months before he was elected into the position, and the fact that she was also dating a Duke herself, made her think she was an *expert* on my love life.

"It's one thing to casually date two guys at once, but I

3

draw the line at sleeping with them at the same time," I replied.

"Unless it literally is *at the same time.*"

My body heated at the idea of being the filling of a Liam and Porter sandwich. I'd fantasized about it, touched myself and climaxed at the mental picture of being in bed with the two virile men. Even did some discreet online shopping for some butt plugs to see what it would be like. What would it be like fucking two men at the same time, one in my pussy, the other in my ass? One dark, the other fair. Big hands meant big dicks, and I squirmed in my seat hoping I'd get to confirm that with them. Hopefully tonight.

"Exactly. So that's why we're meeting at Cassidy's, to tell them that I want to be with them. Together. Enough with casual dating."

"Good, because there's no doubt those two have blue balls."

"You're worried about them? What about me? Have you seen those guys? I've been dating two hotties and haven't gotten more than kissed."

"That's your own making," she countered. "If you'd talked to them about this weeks ago, there's no doubt in my mind you'd have gotten both of them in your bed by now."

I made a funny whimpering sound. A mixture of worry, horniness and agreement. But I still doubted, still worried they'd laugh when I told them the truth. I wasn't used to men committing. My dad had bolted when I was a kid, leaving my mom high and dry to raise two kids on her own in a small town with limited job opportunities. My brother was turning out to be just like him: selfish and irresponsible. Relying on men wasn't something I did. Perhaps that was why it had taken me this long to even attempt to tell Porter and Liam what I wanted. It was easier not to have them in my life, but they weren't anything like men I knew. They were... *good.* Gentlemen through and through.

But if they left like my dad... it would destroy me.

Parker laughed. "Fix it. I've seen the way they look at you. They are into you. Seriously. Give your vibrator a break and go for the real thing. Times two."

Times two sounded fabulous. I'd never been with two guys before. My technique in bed was pretty much limited to missionary and a few other non-Kama Sutra positions. And orgasms? I might have been with a guy or two, but it took a little clit play on my part to get off. Taking on two dicks at once was well beyond my experience level. Just because I hadn't tons of experience didn't mean I didn't fantasize about more... didn't read about it in steamy books. But I wanted to go for it anyway. With Porter Duke and Liam Hogan. I wanted it all with them.

With the engine off, it was getting cold fast, but thoughts of being with those two kept me warm. Kissing them had been thrilling enough. And that had been on the mouth. What could they do to other places on my body? *At the same time?*

Glancing out the window again, I saw Porter walking toward me down the sidewalk. My heart skipped a beat at the sight of him. Big, like block-out-the-sun kind of big. Unlike his cousin, Duke, who was similarly sized and went into the pro rodeo circuit, Porter had gotten a football scholarship to college. He might have left those linebacker days behind him when he graduated and went to law school, but he hadn't lost the size. He didn't wear a coat, even on the coldest of nights, saying he was built like a furnace and never needed one.

His dark hair peeked out from beneath his cowboy hat. He saw me and smiled and even from a distance, I could see his dimple.

God, I had it bad. *Really* bad. I'd never felt like this for anyone else... besides Liam. I'd never been in love before, but it felt a whole lot like it. I had a feeling he was right there with me because the way he looked at me, the way he talked to me... I just wanted to lean into him and hold on, let him take care of me. He wanted more of a commitment than I'd been willing to give, until now. Not that I was a wait-for-marriage kind of gal, because I wasn't, but I'd needed to be sure.

Glancing in the rearview mirror, I saw Liam Hogan coming down the sidewalk from the other direction. God, my heart clenched at the sight of him as well. Laid back and easygoing, the blond had a quick smile and a generous nature. Protective as could be. And he was horrible at bowling. He also had pale eyes that looked at me with such heat that it ruined my panties. And a man in uniform? I was a goner. I loved him, too. God, I did. I wanted to climb in his lap and never get up.

But since I'd been dating both men, I refused to do more than kiss either of them, but when the chemistry was off the charts, it had been soooo hard. It wouldn't be fair to do more with either one and it would feel like cheating. I didn't want to string them along, but I wanted both of them. And tonight, things had to change. No more dating. No more casual.

The men stopped in front of my car, stood shoulder to shoulder and looked at me. I gulped. This was the first time I'd seen them together. They were big, strong guys and they both wanted me. Hopefully, after our little chat, they would continue to do so. I pushed all thoughts of my pain-in-the-ass brother out of my mind.

This was it. I bit my bottom lip to stifle a silly giggle. Two men. I wanted both of them. At the same time. And it was time to tell them.

 ORTER

"She wouldn't make a date with both of us if she were going to dump us. Right?" Liam murmured, tucking his hands in his coat pockets as we stood beside each other on the sidewalk.

It was cold as fuck, but I was hoping before the night was out, we'd be staying warm with Jill between us. Naked. My dick was getting hard just thinking about it. Hell, it had been hard for her for months, ever since we started dating. *Dating.* Shit, that term was a social media status, not reality. Not at my age. Did a thirty-four-year-old *date?*

Reality was Liam and I biding our time until our girl got over the issues she had with being with both of us. Yeah, it was a big deal and not 'normal.' But what the hell was normal when it came to relationships? Hopefully, we were done waiting and we could make it official.

"Hell, no. She's too sweet for that."

I heard Liam offer a grunt in response. "There's more to her than sweet, and I'm ready to bring that out."

"Fuck, yes," I murmured, more to myself than Liam.

Jill Murphy was everything I ever wanted in a woman. Smart, caring, thoughtful, full of integrity and perseverance. She'd worked her way through college to be a nurse, took care of her mother while she'd been sick and had been her brother's guardian after the woman passed away. She deserved to have someone take care of her for a change. Lucky for her, she had two men who wanted to do that.

I'd been friends with Liam for years, but had never considered claiming a woman together until recently. Until we saw Jill here at Cassidy's one night. Then, it was all over. One look at her and I'd been sucker punched right in the gut. No, right in the heart. TKO—total knock out—for me. It had been years since I'd been in a serious relationship and that had been a total clusterfuck. Sierra had not only stomped on my heart, but she'd destroyed my career. I hadn't turned into a monk, but I hadn't expected to be serious about a woman ever again. Until Jill.

Same went for Liam. He saw her and he was done searching. We weren't going to fight over her. Hell no. Why should we? It wasn't like I was the first Duke who shared a woman.

Parker Drew, Liam's predecessor as sheriff, had taken up with my cousin, Gus, and two other men. Sure, the fucker Beirstad had stirred some shit up, but Parker herself had shut that down. So had Auntie Duke.

No one else in town cared, and I didn't give a fuck if they did. No one was going to mess with my career because of a ménage relationship. No, a threesome was no big deal. A woman using me for my position as the DA so her case could be tossed because of conflict of interest—fucking the defendant was definitely that—was a bigger problem. That might have been Sierra, but that wasn't Jill. She was too sweet for that, even if she had an inner vixen who craved two dicks.

Nothing stood in the way of making Jill ours. Except Jill herself. She'd been clear from the beginning that she wanted to date both of us. We knew it, were—grudgingly—fine with it since we hoped it would eventually get her between us. But two months? My hand wasn't enough to satisfy my dick, to empty my balls of all the cum I made just thinking about her.

She refused to do anything more than kiss. Hell, that's all we'd done in the time we'd been *dating*. And that was on the lips. I envisioned getting my mouth on more of her than that. Her dainty collarbone, the full undercurve of her breast, the jut of her hipbone, the inside of her thigh. Her pussy.

I licked my lips, ready to discover how sweet she was *all* over.

The time with her had been more chaste than being in high school; there hadn't even been making out in a car. No hot and heavy petting. No second base.

I ran my hand over the back of my neck. What we'd been doing was courting. Two months of getting to truly know Jill Murphy. Her likes, dislikes. Quirks. The fact she was allergic to grapes, that she worked too fucking hard. The time had been worth it. For me, and Liam had agreed, for him as well. It had only solidified that we wanted her, and not just for a quick fuck. That she was *ours,* that we loved her. We just had to get that smart brain of hers to finally admit it as well.

We'd continue to take things slow and easy with her until she was ready. But I was a red-blooded male and she was hot as hell. I'd dreamed of all kinds of dark and dirty things to do with her. Rubbed one out in the shower often enough—daily —thinking of her. On my bed, naked, thighs spread nice and wide. Bent over the back of my couch. Sprawled out on my kitchen table.

Fuck, I was getting hard just thinking about it.

She wasn't a quick lay. No easy romp with her. Not that I wanted one. No, I wanted forever with Jill. Liam, too. When we took her for the first time—and we would—it wouldn't be chaste. It wouldn't be sweet. It would be wild, but it would be the last first time for all of us. She had to know that once we claimed her, she was ours. Permanently. Perhaps that was why she'd been taking her time. That she knew there would be no going back.

"Who the hell is she talking to?" Liam asked, his breath puffing out in a white cloud.

I didn't respond because how the hell should I know? She didn't look too happy though and *that,* I knew, was what Liam was talking about. Whoever it was had a frown marring her pretty face.

"Bringing our girl down is so fucking wrong," he added.

"Probably her dumbass—and deadbeat—brother," I grumbled.

Liam gave another grunt of agreement. He was more familiar with Tommy Murphy than I was since he'd been picked up a number of times, but had yet to need someone from the District Attorney's office. I knew that was only a matter of time though. He was twenty, no longer a kid and those apron strings connecting him to Jill needed to be cut. With their family history and Jill's kind heart, that was going to be a hard task.

Jill ended her call and we watched as she tossed the cell into her purse and climbed from the car. When she rounded the hood, she smiled at us.

I'd come from work, parked down the block to meet Jill for dinner. Liam had texted me saying he'd gotten the same

11

invite, which gave us both hope. He'd walked from the sheriff's office the next block down.

"That just made my day," I said as she stepped up onto the sidewalk. I held out my hand to help her over a small patch of snow. While she had on mittens, I could feel the heat of her hand through the wool.

She looked up at me with her dark eyes that twinkled in the street lights. Being a foot shorter, she had to tip her head back to look at me. It only reminded me of how fragile she was, although I didn't dare say that to her. She could take care of herself, sure enough. She'd proven that over the years, but why should she have to?

"Oh?" she asked, stepping close.

"Your smile, sweetness." I stroked a finger over her cheek. "Just what I love to see."

Her grin spread across her face and she looked away, suddenly a little shy. Even in the darkness, I could see her cheeks pinken. "That smile isn't just for you, Porter Duke."

Liam took hold of her hand and tugged her gently toward him. He lowered his head and gave her a quick kiss on the lips. "That's right, some of that sugar's for me, too. Right?"

Jill looked up at him, nodded. I wasn't holding my breath, but I felt like my entire body exhaled. It was the first time the three of us had done anything together and the fact that she kissed Liam in front of me was a good sign. Was tonight the night she agreed to share herself with both of us?

"That's our girl," he said, then took her hand. "Everything all right?"

An orange hat covered her head, her dark hair trailing long down her back. With her thick, black coat going down to her knees, I could only see a bit of jeans tucked into boots. No colorful scrubs, so she must have changed at the doctor's office before meeting us.

Her smile slipped a little and she sighed. "Just talking with Parker."

Ah. She'd been working in my office for two months and had tried to stay out of whatever the hell Liam and I were doing with Jill. Not very well. Clearly, she was working on Jill. I just had to hope she was trying to get our girl to admit she was into both of us.

"Talking about good stuff, I hope," Liam said.

"I hope," she murmured, taking a deep breath and smiling brilliantly. "I'm starved."

I nodded, took her hand. "Then let's get you fed."

Then maybe, after we talked and finally got her to admit she wanted both of us, we could get her to my house and feed her something else. Like our cocks.

$\mathcal{L}$IAM

I WAS USED to interrogating suspects, working them for answers, getting them to admit the truth. My knuckles showed the scars from fighting when I was younger, when I liked to use my fists to solve problems. But the badge on my chest considered that kind of dispute resolution illegal, so I got good with my words. As the county DA, Porter was, too. But Jill Murphy wasn't a suspect, and there hadn't been any hard evidence to prove that she wanted us both. Until now.

She'd asked us to meet her for dinner, which she'd never done before. We'd taken her out separately, never together. I'd been bold out on the sidewalk and kissed her, and she'd let me. With Porter watching. She wouldn't have let me do that if she hadn't been okay with it, if it hadn't screamed *I want both of you!*

I had it bad. Completely pussy whipped and I hadn't even had any of her pussy.

Jill was so fucking good. Honorable to a fault. She wasn't sneaky, dating two men secretly. Not that it was possible in a town the size of Raines, but I'd known women to try it. Guys, too. Ended up going on a few domestic calls for just this reason.

But being honorable didn't mean she was all sweet and pure. No woman who wanted two men could be. She had to know what it would be like, that two sets of hands, two mouths, two cocks were better than one.

At twenty-six, she definitely wasn't a virgin. And while all she'd had were kisses the past two months, it didn't mean she didn't dream of more. Didn't slide her hand in her panties and make herself come. Pull a vibrator or big dildo from her bedside table and get off thinking of me and Porter. She could play all she wanted, but it would be nothing like the real thing. I was bigger than any dildo she could buy and while Porter and I had never shared a woman before, I had no doubt he'd ruin her for any battery operated boyfriend.

But the table between us wasn't in an interrogation room. Jill wasn't a suspect. She was my future wife. I wouldn't force the words I wanted from her.

No, she'd give them to me. To us.

I'd never shared a woman before. Never considered it. Not until Jill. Yeah, it might be a little awkward at first getting naked and fucking her with Porter in the room. Hell, in the same bed, and eventually at the same time, but it was all about Jill. We'd been friends long enough, shared enough experiences to know we wanted to make a life with her together.

The scent of burgers made my mouth water and country

music came from the jukebox in the corner. Cassidy's was busy, filled with a lingering happy hour crowd and those who wanted a dinner out. It was too early for the heavy drinkers. I didn't give any of that my attention. I was focused solely and completely on Jill. With her expressive dark eyes, heart-shaped face, full lips and gorgeous brown hair, I couldn't look away.

Jill had been leading things with us up until now. It was time for us to take over. Ironic it was here at Cassidy's since this was the first place I laid eyes on her. The place where I decided she'd be mine. That Porter and I would share her. I glanced at him, and he gave me a slight nod.

We couldn't force a confession, but we could definitely try to coax one from her.

"How was work?" I asked, starting off easy.

Porter and I were too big to fit comfortably in one of the booths along the walls, so we were at a four-top table. We'd piled our outerwear on the empty chair beside her. Her hair was a little mussed from tugging off her hat, but I liked it that way because it made me think of what it might look like after a long night of fucking. Winter clothing didn't show a lot of skin, and Jill's pale pink sweater covered her from neck to wrist. But it didn't hide her soft curves as she sat across from us.

She took a sip of her beer, set the pint glass down on a coaster. "Fine. I'm just glad it's Friday and I can sleep in tomorrow."

I hoped she'd want to sleep in because we'd keep her up learning how soft her skin was, what made her whimper and beg, what she sounded like when she came. Then we'd do it all over again.

"You work too hard," Porter said.

16

Her dark eyes met his and I saw a mixture of agreement and defiance. She shrugged. "I don't plan on working two jobs forever. Trust me." She sighed and rolled her eyes. "A year left on my mother's medical bills, then I'll hit my student loans hard. But that's not important. What about you, did you close that case?"

She looked to me with her usual open and interested gaze, clearly wanting to change the subject. She didn't like to bring up that she was in debt, that she was struggling to stay above water financially, even working close to sixty hours a week. To offer her money would be bad. Really bad. It wasn't like I was rich—being sheriff wouldn't make me a millionaire —but the family ranch was partially mine and I didn't need much. Jill wouldn't take charity, wanting to work for her keep. I respected the hell out of that, but she'd work herself into an early grave if she kept it up. Being with her meant her burdens were our burdens, that she wouldn't have to work so hard. Hell, she wouldn't have to work at all if that was what she desired. It wasn't, I knew, but she could let Porter and I support her.

One thing at a time.

I offered her a nod. "I did. It's in Porter's hands now." As the District Attorney, he would work with the guy's lawyer to either make a deal or take it to court.

His dark brow went up. "The Monroe case?"

Low-level drug dealer caught with a stash of meth in the trunk of his car. Possession. Intent to distribute. "Yup."

"With the evidence against him, it's open and shut," Porter added. "Something to celebrate. Is that why you called to have dinner with both of us? Are we celebrating, sweetness?"

Jed Cassidy came by then with our meals instead of the waitress who had taken our orders. At well over six feet and a retired pro rodeo rider, it was an adjustment seeing him running a bar instead of on the back of a bucking bronc. But, he loved his second career—and there was no chance of breaking his neck—and I couldn't fault him that.

"Good to see you finally claimed these two for yourself, Jill." He winked at her and her cheeks turned a pretty shade of pink.

Her gaze flicked to me, then Porter. She licked her lips, clearly a little nervous.

"You finally got your heads out of your asses and got her between you," Jed continued, glancing our way. He didn't have it right, but I wasn't going to correct him. "Kaitlyn will be thrilled to know you'll all be joining us at some Duke get-togethers."

Jed had claimed Kaitlyn, the town librarian, with Porter's cousin, Duke. Jed, like me, was tangentially connected to the Duke family.

Parker Drew, my old boss and the previous sheriff, had told me all about the Duke dinners. Since she was happily linked to Gus Duke, another one of Porter's cousins—he had four—as well as the other two vets in town, Kemp and Poe, I'd gotten plenty of info on that family.

After the election and I'd taken over her job, Parker had coincidentally taken a position as a lawyer in Porter's office, so I had no doubt she'd probably been pestering him about getting together with Jill. On a daily basis.

As for the Duke weekly get-togethers, I hadn't joined Porter at any of them—he didn't get to every one himself—but I had a feeling we would soon, just as Jed suggested.

Jed set a plate loaded with a cheeseburger and fries in front of Jill. "You're going to make some ladies around here pretty mad taking these two off the market." He angled his head toward us.

"I…" Jill began, continuing to glance between me and Porter. I couldn't help but smile, enjoying how she was flustered. Jed was helping us along without even realizing he was doing so.

He set down Porter's plate next, then mine. "I have to thank you, by the way," he continued, pointing at Jill.

"Oh?" she asked, clearly a little flustered.

"Because of you, I won twenty bucks. Duke figured it would take them another month to claim you."

I should have been insulted, but definitely wasn't.

Jill's mouth hung open and she looked at him wide-eyed. "You bet on me?"

Jed shook his head. "Not you. Them." He hooked his thumb at us.

"Well, Jill?" Porter's words had her turning his way. "Has Jed won twenty bucks?"

I reached out, took her hand. "Have we claimed you?"

I held my breath, waiting for her answer. Porter was a catch. A solid job, owned a house with land, had no real debt, came from a strong, supportive family, had all his hair, and by what the women in town said, was hot as hell. There had always been a little bit of me that wondered, why me, too? What did Jill see in me? I could see her happy with Porter. *Just* Porter. If she wanted us both now, would she change her mind later?

"Wait, I thought it was a done deal," Jed said, but we didn't look his way. He had his girl, it was time for us to get ours.

I stared at Jill, who looked a little panicked and a whole lot nervous. Waited.

"Well?" Porter asked.

"Shit, guys, did I step in it? I'm sorry. But, Jill, tell me I won twenty bucks," Jed added.

As if Jed cared about the twenty bucks. He just wanted to gloat and hold it over Duke.

I didn't hear the music or the chatter of those around us. I didn't even breathe as I waited for the one word I'd longed to hear.

Of course, right then, her cell rang.

4

 ILL

SHIT. Shit! They were asking me, point blank, if I wanted both of them. Jed had even helped me. I'd been so nervous to say the words. *So guys, I happen to want both of you. Not that you're not enough individually, because you're both amazing, but heck, my pussy gets wet for the idea of double dick.*

A guy's ego was only so strong. Would they think I thought less of them because I needed *two* men? Jed had pretty much said I'd claimed them and they hadn't stormed off. In fact, they looked at me with open expressions. Eager ones. As if they were hoping for me to say yes. The moment had come. The answer was on the tip of my tongue, so of course my cell would ring.

"Sorry, I've got to check on this." I tugged my hand from Liam's hold. "A co-worker at the hospital, well, her daughter is having a baby—her second—any day now, and I volunteered to babysit the two-year-old so they can all be with her. I'm on standby."

The men looked at me, didn't say anything. Waited patiently, like usual. Jed offered a small wave and went back to work.

"Hello?"

"Jillian Murphy?" The man's voice on the phone was deep and one I didn't recognize.

"Yes," I replied.

"This is Bob at the Jumping Jack Pawn Shop in Clayton."

All the eagerness I'd had all day for my date with Porter and Liam was gone. The anticipation of answering them with a very blatant yes was shot to hell.

I flicked a look at Liam and Porter, and I held up a finger to tell them this would take a minute.

Why did this have to happen now? *Now!* I had an idea of what the guy was going to say. It was going to be hard to be excited about anything after this because any mention of my brother, Tommy, these days was all bad and always involved another mess for me to clean up. My appetite for a greasy cheeseburger and fries was gone.

"Yes, hi." It was rude that I didn't sound very excited to talk to Bob, but I couldn't help it.

"I'm guessing you know why I'm calling," he replied.

I leaned back in my chair, closed my eyes for a moment. "What did my brother pawn today?"

I held my breath.

"A TV and a rhinestone brooch shaped like a butterfly."

My mother's pin.

I gripped the cell so tight I was sure my knuckles were white. I envisioned it being Tommy's neck.

"While you might want a chance to get your TV back, I figured I'd give you a call about the brooch."

We'd done this once before. Last year, Tommy had taken my mother's silver tea set in and pawned it. I'd discovered it missing when I'd been cleaning. I'd confronted Tommy about what he'd done and raced to the pawn shop in the hopes of getting it back. Fortunately, there wasn't a big rush for tea sets, and it had still been in a display case. He'd been kind and sold it back to me at the amount he'd given Tommy. I had it hidden away now in the linen closet behind the sheets. It wasn't like Tommy ever changed his, or slept on them anymore.

While my twenty-year-old brother still technically lived with me in the house we'd grown up in, I rarely saw him. He'd never had any ambition to go to college. Hell, he'd barely finished high school. He had zero work ethic and held a minimum wage job with a now-familiar irregularity. Most of his time was spent at the casino off the highway. I had no idea where he slept at night.

"Thank you," I told the pawnbroker. I *was* thankful.

My anger morphed into sadness. Yes, the brooch meant something to me. Besides the house and the ancient car I drove, there wasn't much that had belonged to my mother and held sentimental value. I'd had to sell quite a bit to pay for her funeral expenses, and I loved that brooch.

I cleared my throat, but couldn't say anything yet.

"I'll sit it in the back," he continued. "If you want to come in, you can have it for what I gave your brother. Fifty dollars."

Fifty dollars. Tommy was giving away one of the last pieces of our mother for a measly fifty dollars. To do what? Gamble it away at the casino. The money was probably already gone on a hand of blackjack or the spin of the roulette wheel.

"Yes, I'd love it if you'd hold it for me. I can come in

tomorrow." I didn't have extra cash before payday, especially for something like this, but I could take it out of the food budget. It seemed it would be PB&J until next Friday.

I thanked him and ended the call, tossed the cell back in my bag.

I looked up at Liam and Porter. "I've got to go."

Liam frowned. "Stay. Talk to us. Whatever's going on with your brother, we want to hear about it. We want to help."

God, he was so sweet. *They* were so sweet. But this was my problem, my brother. I'd been through this before. Again and again. I couldn't drag them down into this. I knew I wasn't going to be good company, not after that call. It wasn't fair to either of them to ruin their Friday night.

I shook my head, stood. They rose to their feet, too. "You stay. Eat. I'm not in the mood now for company."

"You said he pawned some things but can get them back?"

I nodded, knowing they'd only heard half the conversation, but had recapped it pretty well.

"You're not thinking of going to a pawnshop by yourself, tonight?" Liam asked, putting his hands on his hips. He'd come right from work and wore his uniform shirt. The star on his chest caught the restaurant lighting and reminded me this was Sheriff Hogan asking me this, not just Liam, the man. Both sides of him were ruthlessly protective.

"No, of course not." Tomorrow, I would. It was in Clayton, Montana, not some rundown part of a big city. I'd be fine.

"You're not going to go searching for Tommy?" he added, clearly worried I was going to go off by myself to shady places.

I shook my head. I had no idea where to start with that. He could be anywhere from the casino on the reservation to any bar—besides Cassidy's—in the county, to some low-life's house where he was crashing these days. I was upset, but I wasn't stupid. "I'm going home."

"Sweetness—"

I knew Porter was going to try and talk me out of it, so I lifted my hand, cutting him off. I had to go before I cried. I hadn't cried in years... all the tears had dried up when Mom died, but looking at them, seeing the concern on their faces, made a lump form in my throat. I'd held it together for so long on my own, I wasn't sure if I could handle them right now. I'd fall apart, I knew it. And what then? They'd want me even less. What guy wanted a needy woman?

No, I'd go home, hope Tommy was there, but since I hadn't seen him in two weeks, I highly doubted it. I'd call him, text him, get him to respond. Yell at him. Then get the tub of ice cream out of the fridge and read a book and try to forget.

"Please. I'll... I'll see you both soon."

I avoided looking at them as I grabbed my coat and purse and fled, knowing Tommy had ruined everything.

* * *

ME: *OMG. How could you? That was Mom's pin!*

I TEXTED that to Tommy from the car. When I had no response by the time I got home, I tugged on my flannel pajamas and thick socks, texted him again.

ME: *Where are you? Come home so we can talk.*

· · ·

25

JUST AS I settled onto the couch with a pint of Rocky Road, he texted back.

TOMMY: *Needed quick cash. I'll pay you back.*

I ROLLED my eyes at the phone. Not once, ever, had he paid me back for all the money I'd given him, or for the things he'd pawned or sold. His bedroom was practically bare now since he'd sold everything... somehow. His stereo was gone. Laptop, gone. Even his clock radio had disappeared.

There was no point in texting him again. He wasn't coming home. He wasn't going to apologize. He never had because he didn't think he'd done anything wrong. Not only had he taken one of the last things that was our mother's and hocked it, he'd ruined my night with Porter and Liam. God, they'd asked me outright if I'd claimed them, had been waiting for my answer. Then BAM. Ruined.

I could have stayed at the restaurant with them. They'd wanted me to do so. It had been my choice to leave. Learning what Tommy had done was another sucker punch. He was my brother. Family. Family was supposed to take care of each other, do stuff together, *be* together. Tommy didn't see it that way. I'd been the fill-in parent since Mom died, been his legal guardian, but once he turned eighteen, he'd pretty much checked out.

I could understand if he'd gone off to college across the country. Gone into the military and ended up stationed far away. It was his life and he should go live it. But what he was doing was different and downright cruel.

Still, he was my baby brother, and I wanted so desperately to have it like it used to be. I knew it wasn't going to happen, but that didn't keep me from wishing. Every time he pulled something like this, it just dug that knife in a little deeper.

Tonight was supposed to be me finally telling Porter and Liam I wanted to be with both of them. To hopefully get them to do more than just kiss me. I believed them when they'd said they wanted to know what was going on with Tommy, to listen, and that was great, but that wasn't the point of the dinner date. I hadn't wanted to sit in Cassidy's with them, eat burgers and vent about my problems. They had tough jobs dealing with people who committed horrible crimes. No way did they need to spend their Friday night listening to me complain about how Tommy had gone from a sweet kid to out of control. A gambler. Possibly even worse. I'd tried my best to raise him when Mom died, but clearly I'd done a horrible job.

I jabbed my spoon into my ice cream, took a bite, settled deeper into the couch. I grabbed my book, the steamy romance I'd gotten from the library, and opened it to where I'd left off the night before. After reading two pages of a *funishment* spanking and a sex scene where the woman was happily tied to a bed and brought to the brink of orgasm by the hero licking her pussy, I groaned and tossed it onto the coffee table.

It was possible—if the night had gone differently—I could have had Liam's head between my thighs right now. Or Porter pressing me against the shower wall and filling me up with his huge dick. I could have been in bed… with both of them, getting real man-induced orgasms instead of just reading about it. But no, I was here feeling sorry for myself, sad that Tommy didn't give a shit anymore, that he was throwing his life away.

I steered my thoughts to Porter and Liam. Would they spank me like the heroine in the book? Was that something they liked to do? No one had ever done it to me before, but reading about it made me hot, made me wet. I was here, alone, in my comfortable, yet not sexy, PJs, horny from weeks and weeks of wanting two men and not doing anything about it. Wet between my thighs from reading about the kind of sex I wanted to have. With them.

The only thing I could do about it was take care of this need myself. Just like I did with everything else in my life. I was on my own. I worked my ass off, paid the bills, bought the groceries, took care of my own orgasms.

Settling my feet nice and wide on the coffee table, I slid down on the couch and slipped my hand into the front of my pajama pants. I might not be able to have Liam and Porter tonight, but it didn't mean I couldn't fantasize about them, couldn't call out their names as I slipped my fingers through my slick folds, dipped two inside my eager entrance and rubbed my clit.

5

ORTER

Tommy Murphy was a little shit. I wanted to track him down and have a little chat that involved my fist in his face. But from what Liam had told me on our drive to Jill's house, the punk needed more than that. He needed a broken nose for what he was doing to his sister, followed by some hard work. Real, backbreaking labor that made him learn quickly that there was no get rich quick scheme, no honor or integrity in using a family member like he did Jill.

Our girl had worked her fingers to the fucking bone to take care of him after their mom died. She'd worked full-time while getting her nursing degree to support them both so the state didn't put him into the system. And now? He wasn't a fucking kid anymore. He needed to own his shit, get his priorities straight, like taking care of Jill instead of the other way around. He was a man and needed to start acting like one—one who took care of the women in his life, who respected and honored them.

But dealing with Tommy could wait. Jill couldn't. She might've wanted to be by herself, to close herself off from us, but that wasn't going to happen any longer. We'd given her enough time to get her mind around both of us being her men. It was time to take over, to take control. Liam agreed.

That was why we'd given her an hour on her own and were now climbing the steps to her front porch, ready to ring her doorbell and tell her how it was going to be. A cry broke the cold silence, and I looked to Liam, my senses on alert. This was an older neighborhood, the houses small and spaced nicely apart.

That sound had come from Jill and she was in trouble. I took one step toward the door, ready to break it down if I needed to, but Liam reached out and put his palm on my chest to stop me.

"Porter, yes!"

The muffled words could be heard clearly and my eyes widened. Holy shit. Jill wasn't hurt, she was getting off. And she was calling my name.

Liam peeked in the window to the right of the front door. When his eyebrows went so high as to disappear beneath his cowboy hat, I joined him. The blinds weren't drawn—we'd have to talk to her about that—and we could see in. Our girl was on the couch in the middle of the room, cast in a soft yellow light of the lamp on the table beside her. Her feet were up on the coffee table before her and there was no way to miss her hand inside her pajama pants. I wished I could see how she worked her pussy. Were her fingers fucking that tight hole or just sliding over her wet folds? Was her palm rubbing against her clit or were her fingertips making tiny circles over it?

"Liam, more. Yes, spank me. Harder," she called out as her hips arched up off the couch.

Her eyes were closed, her head pressed back as she bit her lip.

Liam stood beside me, equally transfixed. "Holy fuck," he whispered. He reached down, adjusted himself.

My dick was rock hard, too. I'd never seen anything so erotic in my entire life and Jill was completely covered. She was playing with her pussy and thinking about us. Thinking about us *spanking* her. This would be top of my fantasies I'd jerk off to for a long time.

If there had been any question that Jill wanted both of us, it was answered now. She'd sealed her fate by slipping her fingers into that pussy of hers and shouting our names.

"She's not coming without us," I murmured. While I didn't want to move from the gorgeous sight, the orgasm she was close to having was ours.

"Fuck, yes. She wants to get off, it's our job now to get her there."

I went to her door and knocked. Glancing at Liam who was still watching, he nodded, and I knew she'd stopped her play.

I had no intention of scaring her, someone randomly knocking on her door after dark, so I called, "Jill, it's Porter and Liam. Open the door for us, sweetness."

Liam joined me when the porch light came on.

"What are you doing here?" she asked after she let us in, shut the door behind us.

While we'd both been to her house before for dates, we hadn't been inside. Her entry opened right into her small living room. The space was warm and cozy, but the furniture was dated, probably purchased a long time ago by her mother. I could see into the kitchen; everything was spotless.

She was looking up at us, waiting. The flannel pajama pants and pink fleece pullover she wore weren't the least bit sexy, but knowing what she'd done in them, that her pussy was all warmed up and wet beneath the soft fabric had me reaching out, taking her right hand and holding it up. She blushed and her eyes widened. She must have wiped her fingers on her pants before answering the door, but she hadn't gotten all the pussy juice that glistened there. I leaned down, lifted them to my mouth and sucked on her wet pointer and middle fingers.

I could smell her musky scent even as her sweet flavor burst on my tongue. Pre-cum spurted from my dick. I was in trouble here, ready to come like a horny teenager just from a taste of her sweet flavor, and not from the source.

"After the call you got, we wanted to make sure you were okay," Liam said. "But now, we're going to make sure you get that orgasm you were working on."

I let her hand go and smiled.

"I don't know what... I mean—" We had her all flustered and turned on. No question she had an idea now of what my tongue would feel like on her pussy, flicking over her clit.

"Sweetness, I just licked your pussy juices off your fingers," I said.

Liam went to her window, tugged on the cord and lowered the blind. "Close these at night, Jill. No one sees you playing with yourself but us."

Her eyes darted to what he was doing and quickly understood she'd been caught. We didn't want her feeling embarrassed or have any shame about pleasuring herself; a woman was allowed to enjoy her body and we certainly loved watching her do just that. But Jill didn't need to take care of her orgasms herself; we'd do that for her from now on.

"We heard you call out our names as you played with your pussy. You don't need to fantasize, sweetness. You can have the real deal. You want both of us?"

I held my breath, waited as she looked at us. Nodded. "Yes," she said.

Exhilaration pumped through my veins along with the caveman need to claim, to get that pussy juice all over my mouth, my fingers, my dick. I wanted to be marked.

"This isn't a fling, Jillian Murphy," Liam said. His voice was soft, but the tone deep. "This isn't you having some fun with two dicks. We aren't a one-night-stand to fulfill a threesome fantasy. You get between us and there's no going back."

Thankfully, he had a clear mind to tell her how this was going to be. All my thinking was happening with my other head. In my pants. Liam was right. Once we got in that pussy of hers, she belonged to us. Actually, she already did. She had since we picked her up for our first dates. I hadn't felt like this for someone in years. And now, I could see what I'd *thought* was the real deal with Sierra years ago had been far from it. Jill was *The One.* But, we wanted to be clear with her right from the start, so there was no confusion. So she knew we meant forever. So once she said yes again, she was ours.

Licking her lips, she tipped her chin up even further. "I... I understand. I want to be with you, Liam, and you as well, Porter." Absently, she tucked her hair behind her ear. "I always have, but I didn't know how to tell you, if you'd think there was something wrong with me, that I was—"

I put my finger over her lips to silence her. "If you say anything other than that you are perfect, I'll take you over my knee and spank your ass."

Her eyes widened and her pupils dilated.

Liam chuckled. "Our girl likes that idea. No, you need it,

33

don't you? Need to let go and forget everything because you have a stinging ass?"

Yeah, she did. I had to wonder if she'd let some guy do it to her before or if it was, perhaps, something she'd heard about from Parker. No doubt her men reddened her ass often enough. Same went for my other cousins and their women.

I leaned down, kissed her. This time, it wasn't chaste. It wasn't sweet. She gasped at the boldness of my mouth and I swept my tongue inside. Cupping the back of her neck, I gently tugged at her hair and she gasped.

Fuck. I had to stop or I'd take her right here on the floor. "Where are your keys, sweetness?"

She frowned, her eyes blurry from the kiss. "My keys?" She pointed to the small table beside the front door and a little bowl that held a pair of sunglasses and her keys.

Liam scooped them up.

"You have the weekend off and you're spending it with us," I told her. "At my house."

She looked down at herself. "I can't go in my pajamas! I need clothes."

"That's funny. Don't you think so, Liam?" I asked.

He grinned, then leaned down to have his turn kissing her. His hand cupped her jaw to keep her right where he wanted her. When he lifted his head, her lips were a dark pink and glistening, no doubt just like her lower ones between her lush thighs.

"If you think you'll be wearing clothes when you're with us, we're not doing this right," he said. "We're going to Porter's house, getting you naked and learning every sweet, soft inch of your body. Then we're going to make you come. Not once, not twice, but again and again until you forget your own name."

I grunted, thinking of how she was going to look all sweaty and sated in my bed. "Then we're going to fuck you," I added. "All night long."

"Hell, all weekend," Liam clarified. None of us had to work until Monday and we planned to take advantage of every free minute.

She licked her lips again and said, "Oh my."

Leaning down, I scooped her up into my arms. Liam opened the door and I carried her to my SUV, settled her into the middle beside me. I'd just clicked her seatbelt around her as Liam climbed in. He held up her keys and a paperback. "Locked up nice and tight. And this is some interesting reading I found when I turned off the living room lamp."

From the glow of the cabin dome light, I could pretty much bet it was a steamy romance based on the scantily clad couple on the cover.

Jill blushed. Liam offered her a wicked smile as he took his hat off, sat it in his lap.

"This is kidnapping, you know," she told him, although I could hear the playful tone of her words.

"That's only if you don't want to be with us. Last chance, sweetness. Do you want to?" I turned her head toward me, tipped up her chin, kissed her again.

"Yes, I'll come with you," she said once I lifted my head.

"Oh sweetness, you'll come," I replied, putting the truck into gear and driving off. "We guarantee it."

$\mathscr{J}$ILL

WHEN I REALIZED they'd seen me on the couch touching myself, and even worse, heard me crying out their names as I'd fantasized about being with them, I'd wished the ground had swallowed me up. But when Porter had sucked on my fingers—my *sticky* fingers—all thoughts fled. That, holy shit, *that* had been erotic. Sexy as hell. It totally blew my mind and made me realize perhaps they were just as kinky, just as horny as I was.

And now I was between them in the front seat of Porter's huge SUV. I'd been close to coming when they'd knocked on the door. Combining that arousal with the finger licking and then the kisses… I squirmed. My pussy was wet. My pajama pants definitely had a wet spot. My nipples were hard points.

I was relieved they wanted me. And they wanted me… a lot. Liam had blatantly adjusted himself when he'd settled beside me. All my fears had been for nothing, just like Parker had said. We were headed to Porter's house, and they'd very thoroughly described how things were going to go.

Orgasms. Lots of them. Followed by fucking and probably even more orgasms.

I squirmed some more as Porter's garage door opened and he pulled in, shutting off the engine.

The automated door lowered behind us, and we were in a little warm cocoon with only the opener's overhead light brightening the interior.

"You're squirming a lot. What's the matter, sweetness? Is your little pussy eager for some attention?"

Was it? Duh.

I wanted to deny the truth so they didn't think I was so needy. To keep them from thinking I was a slut. But I wasn't a slut. I was a woman who had needs and Porter and Liam had clearly stated they wanted to take care of them. And then some.

Instead, I gave in to what I'd wanted to say for months. "Yes. My pussy aches for both of your big dicks." Bold? Hell yes. But they were offering, and I was going to take.

Liam groaned as he unclipped my seat belt, then his. "Work those pajama pants down over your hips."

"Here?" I asked on a little squeak.

"Right here," Porter added. It seemed he couldn't wait a second longer to see me and watch me come. "We're gentlemen, sweetness. But we know you've got dirty desires in you and we'll take care of each and every one. It's our job now."

I had a feeling those words went a little deeper than just an orgasm, but now wasn't the time to consider. The fact that they couldn't wait a second longer made me even hotter. So I tucked my thumbs into the waistband and worked the loose flannel lower, then lifted my hips to get it past my butt.

I wasn't wearing any panties.

Liam grabbed my right leg, lifted it up and over his muscled thigh, spreading me wide. Porter followed and they worked my pants lower and then off, careful not to take my cozy socks with them. With my legs up and parted, it forced me to slide down into the seat a little so I was leaning back much like I had on my couch earlier. My fleece top didn't cover my lower half. At all.

"Fuck," Porter murmured.

Their hands rested lightly on my inner thighs. The comparison of their ruggedness, their size in comparison to my pale skin, was blatant. They were so manly. Virile. I felt... feminine and strangely powerful even though both of them were a foot taller and weighed at least eighty pounds more.

Liam breathed deeply. "Fuck, I can smell your sweet pussy."

I tried to close my legs, but their hands kept me wide. I wasn't sure if that was a positive thing or not.

"She does smell sweet. Wait 'til you taste her," Porter told Liam. "Like honey."

Liam grunted in response.

I closed my eyes because I'd never had anyone talk about me like this. Like I was the only meal around.

I bit my lip. While I wasn't a virgin, most of the sex I'd had had been Tab A into Slot B kind of sex. Not much looking, but lots of fucking.

Neither was touching me intimately, just looking. And looking.

I hadn't seen very many other women naked, not more than at the gym and then it obviously wasn't up close. My pussy wasn't a neat little slit. My inner lips were large and exposed, a darker pink than what was always described in a romance novel. I'd heard ridiculous terms like meat curtains, but never considered it more than just a funny term.

But now... with two guys, they'd surely seen a fair amount of pussies up close and *very* personal. Did I compare? Would they be turned off?

I squirmed again, this time with doubt.

"You're gorgeous, baby," Liam said. "Look at that pussy."

"I'm big," I blurted.

"Big?" Porter asked, his hand sliding up and down my left thigh, getting closer and closer to my pussy with each pass, but not touching.

"My lips... there. It's kind of ugly."

Liam chuckled. "Baby, that's not a nice way to talk about my pussy."

"*Our* pussy," Porter clarified. "And I agree with Liam. You're perfect. Touch yourself, sweetness. Show us what makes you feel good."

They weren't bothered, didn't run away screaming, so perhaps my complex was just that, completely irrational. I relaxed back into the seat—when had I become tense?—and slid my hand between my parted thighs. I'd never done this in front of anyone before, but I was so hot for them, so hot to come since I'd gotten myself all worked up and then they'd knocked on the door. Left me hanging.

Heat spread as I slid over my clit, circled my entrance.

"See how those pussy lips wrap around your finger? More to get around my dick," Liam told me.

I whimpered as I worked myself up, rubbing my clit with the tips of my fingers in small circles, just how I liked. Heat spread from my fingertips and out over the rest of my pussy. I was getting wetter. My legs tensed, my breath caught. My eyelids fell closed and I felt their hands on my thighs, listened to their dark and dirty promises of what they'd do once I came and I was close.

So close.

Their hands moved, and I felt fingers find my entrance, then slip inside. My eyes popped open and I looked down. My hand on my clit, both men's hands lower. *Both* had a finger in me. They stretched me open, filled me and somehow curved over my g-spot.

"Oh my god," I cried out, not taking my eyes off my pussy as I came. It was as if they'd pushed the orgasm button and there was nothing to do but enjoy.

I'd never come so hard before in my life. Perhaps it was because it was both of them helping me get off. Two men. Both inside me. Both being squeezed and clenched by the pulsing walls of my pussy.

"Good girl. So pretty in your pleasure."

"Fuck, I'm going to come just from the feel of her squeezing my finger."

"She just dripped all over my hand."

"Hot and wet. I can't wait to sink my dick into all this tight heat."

They kept dirty talking as I slowly came back to earth, back to being in Porter's SUV in his garage.

We *still* hadn't made it to a bed. They were *still* dressed. I *still* hadn't seen, felt, been fucked by their big dicks.

Liam slipped his finger from me, lifted it to his mouth and had his turn tasting me.

"Fuck, Porter's right. Like honey."

"More," I gasped. "God, I need more."

I did. So bad.

While that had been incredible, it wasn't nearly enough. I needed to be fucked. Hard and deep. Slow and easy. On my back, riding on top. From behind. I needed it all.

7

*L*IAM

I'D NEVER COME in my pants before. Never got turned on enough, even as a teenager, to blow my load too early. But now, with Jill? There had to be a big wet spot on the front of my jeans for all the pre-cum that was practically dripping from my dick.

Two months of dating had been foreplay. Oh, I'd busted a nut on a daily basis—sometimes twice a day—to relieve the ache in my balls just thinking about Jill. Remembering the feel of her lips as I'd kissed her, the soft scent of her perfume, the lilt of her laugh, the lush swells of her breasts beneath her tops, the fucking sway of her wide hips.

Feeling how tight her pussy was, how soaked it was for us was too much. And when we got to watch her come, to feel her walls clench around my finger, had me on the brink.

And that had been with Porter's finger deep inside her,

too. This was the first co-fucking I'd ever done. Another man's finger was touching mine in a woman's pussy. It should have freaked me out, but it didn't. Not at all. Not because I was hot for Porter, not in the slightest, but because the two of us were getting her off together. We were a team and our mission now was to keep Jill happy, satisfied, sated and as cherished as possible.

If she wanted both of us, we weren't going to hold back. The celibate ship had sailed.

"I can walk, you know," Jill said as I followed Porter through his house and into his bedroom.

I'd scooped her from the SUV and tossed her over my shoulder, bare ass in the air. I held her upper thighs tight so she wouldn't fall. With my free hand, I gave her a light spank.

She giggled, which made me smile and I had to admit, feel ridiculously like a Neanderthal. It was the closest thing to grabbing her hair and dragging her deep into my cave. It had been a long time since I'd felt like this. I'd felt giddy like a seventh grader when Jill had said she wanted to date. When I got my head around Porter and I claiming her together, I became hopeful. I'd been patient, biding my time as we let her work through it all in her head. But there'd always been a niggling doubt that she'd choose to be with Porter, and only Porter.

It had been a rough year with my father dying. My brother, Carson, ran the ranch and I lived there, too. When I'd been a deputy, it hadn't been too hard to work both the land and the law, but being elected sheriff, Carson knew my focus was elsewhere. My dad had held the position for over a decade and I had big shoes to fill. Even though he wasn't around to see me elected, I wanted to make him proud. But that focus had shifted even more once I saw Jill for the first time.

And now, I felt like I had it all. She wanted both of us. In this moment, I didn't doubt. Hell, both our fingers had been in her pussy getting her off. She wouldn't have allowed that if she weren't into us together. She'd said the words. I believed her. But a double finger fuck and now tossed bare assed over my shoulder?

Oh yeah, Jillian Murphy was mine.

Porter's, too, but my dick was screaming *mine!*

Porter flicked on the light switch, two lamps on either side of his huge bed came on. The light was soft, but not too dark. I wanted to take in every inch of Jill's gorgeous body. He turned and his eyes flared, taking in her upturned ass. No doubt he could see her pussy, even with her thighs pressed together.

And what she'd said in the SUV? Oh, she was going to rid herself of any pussy hang ups before the night was over. So she didn't have a little porn star pussy, all pale pink and hidden between a tight slit. Each woman was different and Jill's was as unique as she was. The darker color, the full lips, even the way her clit was always exposed. Didn't she know that was the best way? I could drop to my knees and flick that clit with tongue without going hunting. And those full lips? Fuck, yes, they'd wrap around my dick. And there was more to lick, more to get covered in all that sweet, sticky honey.

Shit, more pre-cum spurted from me. Lowering her to the ground, I held onto her arm until she got her bearings, then opened the button on my jeans, lowered the zipper.

I sighed, my dick thankful for the room.

She stood before me, watched. I arched a brow and tucked a finger beneath the hem of her soft shirt. "Off."

Porter moved to stand behind her, and as she lifted it over

43

her head, he helped her work it off her arms, then dropped it to the floor.

No fucking bra.

I had to close my eyes for a moment at the sight of her. I wasn't going to last. Sheer perfection. She was so much smaller than either of us. Dainty, even. Her breasts were full, not a handful but plump teardrops. Her nipples were large and tightened being exposed to the cooler air. And lower, between her thighs, her gorgeous pussy. She wasn't bare like some women went for these days, but shaved so that there was a small dark thatch, trimmed short, above those plum-toned lower lips. She looked so fucking natural, so real.

"Have you ever done this before?" she asked, glancing up at both of us.

Porter tilted his head. "You mean a threesome?"

She nodded. I couldn't have a conversation while the woman of my dreams stood before me. Naked. So I reached out, cupped a breast. Tested its weight, softness, the stiff peak.

Her breath came out in a breathy exhale and Porter matched my movements with his own hand.

She glanced down at our hands on her. The difference had been striking when we had our hands between her parted thighs in the SUV, but now that we could see every inch of her, completely bare while we were still fully dressed... fuck.

"No," he said. "You?"

She gave a little laugh, but it turned into a whimper when I tugged on her nipple. Those pink tips were remarkably sensitive. "God, no. I want to touch you," she all but whined, but her eyes fell shut and she arched her back so her breasts filled our palms even more.

I dropped my hand, stripped. When I almost tipped over

tugging off my boot, her laughter filled the room. I moved to sit on the ottoman that went with a big comfortable chair to work it off. "Sassy girls get spanked," I said, looking up at her.

She bit her lip, rubbed her thighs together.

Porter swatted her butt. While the crack of it filled the room, it wasn't all that hard. She gasped and squirmed some more. "I'm not sassy, I'm… I'm—"

"Sexy," Porter finished.

"Horny," she countered.

It was our turn to laugh. We couldn't argue with that.

Once I was completely bare, I put my hands behind me on the back edge of the ottoman, leaned back. With my legs out in front of me, my dick jutted lewdly up in the air. I couldn't miss the way her eyes widened as she took it in. I knew she couldn't miss the pre-cum that slid off the crown and down the length.

"Touch away, baby. I'm all yours."

She came up to me, stood between my spread knees. The difference in our height was fixed with me sitting down. She, in fact, was a little taller, but I didn't mind. Her breasts were right in line with my mouth, so I leaned forward and took one between my lips, sucked.

Her fingers went to my hair, tangled.

The soft, silky feel of her skin against my tongue was heaven. The hard peak pressing against the roof of my mouth. The way her body squirmed as I sucked and tugged, licked and even nipped lightly.

"Liam," she breathed. "I want you in me. Now."

"Sweetness thinks she's in charge," Porter said from behind her back.

I lifted my head and glanced at him. He'd stripped off everything but his jeans, which were open, the fly undone. The top of his dick peeked out from the open V.

45

"I'm ready," she added, running her fingers through my hair, over my jaw. A soft touch, but I felt her need in the motions.

"We haven't even warmed you up," I said. "We've got big dicks, baby, and we don't want to hurt you. Just because your pussy's needy doesn't mean it's ready."

"I'm warmed up," she countered, stepping closer, but moving so she straddled one of my bent legs. She sat down on my hard thigh, began to rub her clit against me. Her juices coated my skin and she moved easily.

Fuck, that was hot. Her breasts swayed as she worked herself on my leg.

I tugged her back up to standing. "Check her, Porter."

I wasn't used to telling another man what to do while I was naked, but Porter didn't complain, just cupped her pussy from behind. I watched as his fingers slipped into her, disappeared nice and deep. She went up on her tiptoes as her hands settled on my shoulders for balance.

Wet sounds filled the room as he worked her. But he wasn't touching her clit. I wasn't sure if she was orgasmic without clit contact, but it was sure as shit hot to watch as she rode my friend's fingers.

He pulled them out. "Soaked."

"Please," she whimpered.

Porter handed me a condom. I hadn't been paying him any attention while I had my mouth full of soft tit, but he must have gotten it from a drawer. Somewhere. Hell, who cared as long as I was able to protect Jill and get in her?

I ripped open the packet, but she stilled my hands, climbed up in my lap so she was straddling my legs.

"Whoa, baby."

While I was barely thinking, my dick getting too close to her pussy to do so, I had enough brain cells to slow her roll.

"I gotta protect you."

She shook her head, rolled her hips so that her pussy brushed against the length of me, her breasts rubbing against my chest as she hooked her hands around my neck. "Bare. Take me bare. I've got an IUD."

I groaned, gritted my teeth. I'd never gone without a condom before. Ever. Women had said something similar before, that they were clean and on some kind of birth control. While I believed them, I'd never risked it in case they weren't telling the truth, if they were trying to trap me. I wanted kids, but not that way. Not by deceit. And any woman willing to do that wasn't mother-material in my mind.

I knew Jill wasn't like that, wouldn't lie. I trusted her words. Still…

While I desperately wanted to fuck Jill raw, this was a big fucking deal. Literally. I was clean, there was no question of that. But there was definitely a chance we'd make a baby if she wasn't on birth control. It wasn't that I didn't want kids with her, hell, thinking of her belly all round with our child made me practically lose the last shreds of control I had left.

But we hadn't talked about it and my dick two inches from heaven wasn't the time to do so. We should have done it earlier when we'd been dressed. So much for that.

Porter moved to stand at the side of the ottoman so he could look down at her.

"We said before that there was no going back. But this, sweetness? No condom means forever."

"With both of us," I added, making sure she understood. She was naked in *my* lap, so she probably got that idea. "I'm clean. Got tested as part of the physical for work."

"I am, too. Tested over the summer and I haven't been with anyone since," Porter added. I didn't follow Porter's sex life before we laid eyes on Jill, but I knew there was no other woman my dick wanted.

She looked to Porter, then to me, didn't say anything but shifted over me so the head of my dick slipped through her slick folds, settled into the notch of her entrance.

"I understand. I get tested at the hospital twice a year, and it's been a *really* long time since I've had sex. I've had the IUD for a while."

I didn't want to even think about her with anyone else, but she hadn't asked about our pasts, and I was going to respect hers. She was with us now and that was what mattered.

"I want nothing between us. Not any longer," she breathed. Leaning in, she kissed my chest.

Before she could lower herself down, I gripped her hips, held her up.

"What—"

She was so small it was easy to spin her about so she was still on my lap, but facing away from me.

"Liam!" Her hands settled on my knees to hold on.

"I'll fuck you, don't worry your pretty little head about that. But you're fucking two men now and you need to let Porter watch as you take my dick. As your gorgeous tits bounce while you ride me like a fucking cowgirl."

Porter moved and settled on the edge of the bed facing us. He was too far away to reach her, but had the perfect view.

In this position, perched on my thighs, her feet didn't touch the floor. As I gripped her hips and lifted her up and back and onto my dick, she had no control. She was all mine.

Her hips wiggled as the first inch slipped inside. Fuck, she was tight. Wet. So hot. A whimper escaped and I felt her inner walls flutter, adjusting to being stretched open. I wasn't small. Hell, it was hard to find pants that hid my size, even when I wasn't hard.

I had no doubt her pussy would take me, but it was important I took my time getting her to open up, to be molded to my dick.

It took a minute of raising her up, lowering her down, a shimmy of her hips as I did so, until she was sitting directly on my thighs once again, this time, impaled on my dick.

"Fuck, you're so perfect."

The need to come built at the base of my spine. I'd never been surrounded by such perfection before. Like a snug glove made just for me. I gritted my teeth as I fought for control. I had no idea the difference it was without a condom. Hotter, wetter, more sensitive. Just the idea of being bare deep inside her was so fucking erotic. And the feelings, holy shit, intense. Incredible.

"Ready for your ride?" I asked, sweat beading my upper lip.

I couldn't see her face, but she was circling her hips, trying to lift up. I helped her but raising her so that just the tip was inside, then let gravity lower her back down. Hard. Deep.

She cried out.

I glanced at Porter, who'd tugged his dick from the opening of his jeans and was stroking it. He wasn't missing any bit of her as she was fucked. The way her pussy took all of me, the way her tits did bounce each time she settled back on my lap. The wet, naughty sounds of fucking, of flesh slapping flesh. Or the scent, the musky tang of fucking.

It should feel weird having him watch, but it was too good. *Jill* was too good. I felt pride knowing that he could see her like this, getting what she needed. It was a thrill to show her off, so someone else could appreciate how magnificent our girl was.

I had a moment's thought he might step in front of her and have her suck him off, but she was bouncing too much, and I had a feeling he was enjoying the show. His turn would come, and since I was so close to the edge, it would be soon. But I had to get her off first. The woman *always* came first.

"Liam!" she gasped as I began to fuck her harder. With her legs spread wide, she had no friction on her clit, and I knew she was close, but was struggling to get there.

I wanted her to come with me. I sure as fuck wasn't leaving her behind.

It was easy to continue to lift and lower her with one hand as I reached around and pinched her clit with the other. She came like a firecracker in one silent boom.

A gush of pussy juices seeped from her, coating my dick and my balls. Her thighs clenched tight, her back arched and her inner walls began to milk my dick.

I couldn't survive that. It was impossible, and I wasn't even willing to try. I felt my balls tighten, my dick thicken and shoot a big load deep into her. I filled her with cum, and knowing there wasn't a barrier to collect it, that it coated and marked her deep inside, only made me come even harder.

She leaned back against me, worn out, her head tucked into my shoulder, her breath fanning my sweaty neck. I could look down the length of her body, see the way her nipples softened to plump tips now that she'd come. Lower, to the groomed curls and even further to the way her pussy lips were parted around my base.

My cum slipped from her and there was no way in hell I was going soft. I could take her again, especially knowing that I didn't have to pull out to dispose of a condom. All I had to do was begin again, give her more of my cum. My balls were far from empty.

But it was Porter's turn, and it was time to share. I wasn't the least bit jealous because I sure-as-shit was going to watch. Jill wanted more? She was going to get it.

All fucking night.

 ILL

HOLY SHIT. I'd never come like that before. Ever. It made the orgasm in Porter's SUV seem like nothing, and that was saying a lot. Liam was huge. God, so big I felt crammed full, and I was stunned I'd been able to take all of him. The feel of his dick with no condom had made it even better. The friction, the glide, the feel of his cum as it spurted into me, hot and thick.

It wasn't just Liam. It was seeing Porter in front of me. Watching. Knew he was getting off seeing me be fucked by his friend. Porter had stroked his own dick as Liam lifted me up and down. Taking me, hard, deep. *So deep.*

And watching Porter as I came because of Liam's dick, Liam's fingers on my clit… amazing.

Liam's hand wrapped around my waist, cupped my breast

as he nuzzled against my neck. "Go see Porter, baby. He needs you. Look at his dick, all hard and ready for you."

Through orgasm-hazed eyes, I saw that his cock was almost angry looking, the head a plum color as pre-cum seeped from the slit. While Porter was still idly stroking it, clearly he needed more. He needed to be in my pussy.

I leaned forward and Liam stretched out his legs so my feet were able to touch the ground. I stood slowly, Liam slipping from me as he did so. He patted my ass as I walked toward Porter.

Boldly, I leaned forward and licked the pre-cum from him.

"Fuck!" shouted Porter as Liam growled. I knew he could see my pussy, probably all flushed, swollen and covered in his cum as I bent over.

Porter's taste burst on my tongue. Salty and tangy. I wanted more, but before I could lick him like a lollipop, he gripped my hips, picked me up and tossed me onto the bed. After bouncing once, then twice, he grabbed my ankle and rolled me onto my stomach.

I couldn't help but laugh at how easily he moved me about. I came up on my elbows, looked over my shoulder at him. His hands came down on my bottom with a light swat.

"Sweetness, you're a little tease."

I grinned, because he was smiling as he said it. "Fucking yourself on Liam's cock and getting off while I watch. Then, fuck, then getting that sweet mouth on my dick. I'm close to coming as it is."

I looked down at his dick, which was so big, so thick I was now questioning how I was going to suck him off. I'd have to stretch my mouth so wide just to get the head in. No way could I take the whole thing. Beneath his glorious length were balls, hanging heavy and full, making me think him even more potent, more virile than ever.

"You like seeing me fuck Liam," I said.

"Hell, yes." He swatted my ass again, then cupped it. The sting morphed into heat that spread to my pussy. "And now, with your legs parted like that, I can see he's been there, his cum dripping from you."

I rolled back over, set my feet on the bed, my knees bent. "Mark me, too."

A growl rumbled from his chest as the heat in his eyes went almost predatory.

He moved onto the bed on his knees, took hold of my ankles in one hand, lifted them up to his shoulders. My ass was off the bed because he was so big.

"Like this. I'm going to take you like this."

I wasn't going to argue. I was ready for him and as he leaned forward, gripping his cock in his free hand, he swiped the tip up and down my folds, coating the tip, then settling into place. His dark eyes met mine as he pressed forward.

"Liam's cum is easing the way," he said through gritted teeth. He was going slow because... god, he was big. Finally, he bottomed out and he stilled. Didn't move.

"I never knew it could feel this good. You're perfect, sweetness. Made for my dick. For Liam's. This is going to be fast." His jaw clenched as he pulled back, thrust deep. "Watching you with him was too much. After two months, I'm in you. So hot. So tight. Wet. Shit, I'm going to come."

He fucked me, hard, deep. I gripped the bedding to hold on, not that I was going anywhere as he held my ankles. All I could do was feel, give over to the pounding. It was raw, wet, the sounds of fucking and ragged breathing filled the room.

I watched Porter as he took me, as he found his pleasure in my body. He touched my clit with his free hand, stroked it gently and that was all it took to push me over the edge. Again.

I screamed, arched my back as Porter came with me, buried deep. I could feel his cum filling me, heating me, seeping out around him. There was so much… too much that I felt it slide down over my bottom.

He lowered my legs, leaned forward so his hands were on either side of my head and kissed me. Slow, easy, his tongue tangling with mine. He was still buried deep, still hard.

When he lifted his head, looked at me, he smiled. "There's my girl. I've been dreaming of the look on your face. Well-fucked, happy. Mine."

"Ours," Liam said, coming up beside us with a wet washcloth in his hand. He must've gone to the bathroom and gotten it to clean me up.

"She doesn't need that yet. I'm not done yet."

He may have just come, but he pulled back, thrust deep. Still hard and ready for more.

"Right, sweetness? Why get all cleaned up when I'm going to get you all dirty again?"

I closed my eyes as he lowered to his forearms, moved slow and deep, my clit rubbing against him. This wasn't going to be fast or urgent, but easy. Gentle. Deep.

"Porter, yes." As I wrapped my legs around his thighs, pulled him closer as best I could, he slid over a spot deep inside me that lit me up. Made me hot. Made me scream.

"Yes!"

Why would I want to be clean when I loved being so, so dirty?

9

ILL

MONDAYS WERE USUALLY busy in the recovery room. Planned surgeries began bright and early, so the beds were full by nine. It kept me on my feet, checking on the patients, monitoring their pain, vitals until they were stable and moved on to a room on one of the floors to recover fully. It kept my mind busy, but my thoughts veered from blood pressures and chart updates to Porter and Liam.

I wasn't much for going to the gym and working out, but I would have to consider it if I wanted to keep up with my men. *My men!* They'd been insatiable all weekend. So had I, and I was sore because of it. There were muscles I didn't even know I had that were screaming at me today, reminding me of what we'd done.

But I wasn't complaining. I couldn't help but smile. I'd lost track of how many orgasms I'd had. My co-workers gave me odd looks—no one was as cheerful as I was so early on a Monday—but didn't question. I'd been grilled by Parker on Saturday, although only by text since I'd wanted to give her an update after our phone call in the car Friday night, but not too much more than that as I hadn't been ready to share. I still wasn't, content to just… revel in the feeling of being wanted. No, more than that. I'd been *needed* by two men.

Needed in bed, in the shower, on the kitchen counter. The list of places we'd had sex had been long.

Spending the weekend with Porter and Liam had been everything I'd hoped for. Sex, talking, more sex, cooking and just being together. Oh, and more sex. They'd gone with me on Saturday to the pawnshop to buy back my mom's pin, insisting I wouldn't go alone, but otherwise we'd stayed inside Porter's house. Naked.

I'd only gone home for a few minutes this morning to shower and grab a quick breakfast before I drove to the hospital for my shift. It wasn't even lunchtime and I missed Porter and Liam. It was totally crazy and slightly dangerous. I hadn't realized how lonely I'd been until now. My usual Friday night with a book or a sappy made-for-TV movie seemed dull now. I didn't want a man—men—to make my life exciting. I didn't want to think that I wasn't… whole without them in it. Once I did, I'd be reliant on them. As soon as I did that, I kept myself open for heartache. But I couldn't resist Liam and Porter, and I'd certainly tossed those fears to the side while I'd been with them.

I hadn't done anything except have fun and enjoy myself the entire time.

When I came out of the elevator after wheeling a patient down to a room on the second floor, I was surprised to see Liam. My heart skipped a beat, making me think I needed to get hooked up to a cardiac monitor.

He was at the nurses station chatting with a few people, and I paused, taking a moment to admire him. He was in his usual work uniform of boots, jeans and the sheriff uniform shirt that peeked out from his jacket. To say he filled it out really well was an understatement. Broad shoulders were clearly defined, even beneath the fluorescent lighting. The utility belt around his waist held handcuffs, a walkie talkie and on his hip, a gun. I wasn't big on weapons, but I knew Liam had a big one and knew how to fire it.

God, I was so cliché, but he fit every romance book's sexy sheriff hero I'd ever read about and the hat that rested on the high counter beside him only checked the cowboy box, too. I knew what that mouth felt like on my skin, the gentle touch of those big hands as they worked me to orgasm, the feel of that taut ass beneath my palms. He made me feel giddy. Excited. Eager. Aroused. My nipples hardened beneath my scrub top, and I was thankful for my long sleeved t-shirt and padded bra to hide my obvious attraction. But we were in the hospital and not any place I could act on my desires.

I'd seen him in the building before; work often brought him to see patients or talk with staff about a case. His turf was more the emergency room or even the morgue, but never in the recovery room. I had to wonder if someone had been seriously hurt as part of a crime.

I took a deep breath, let it out and walked toward him, trying not to look as if I'd spent the whole weekend riding his dick and wanted another go.

When he saw me, his eyes brightened, but he didn't offer me more than a small smile. We hadn't talked about how we were going to behave in public—not that I didn't want to jump into his arms and rip the buttons on his shirt off—but this was my work and our relationship was separate from that. So was his.

"Hey there, Sheriff," I said, returning his smile.

He nodded a hello, but Barbara, the head nurse, spoke. "Jill, the sheriff would like to talk with you for a minute." She pointed toward the staff lounge.

My smile slipped as Liam picked up his hat and led me down the hall, holding the door for me. He closed it behind him, but while we were alone, didn't step close. I didn't have a good feeling, as if something wasn't exactly right. He could have been in the building for work and decided to come up and say hello, but he wouldn't need to get Barbara involved for that. Nor would he show up to break up with me. Would he? Had he planned all along to have a wild weekend and then dump me? My nerves had me thinking irrationally because that wasn't something Liam would do. Not after what we shared.

"I wanted to see you this morning, but not for a reason like this," he began.

I worried my lower lip between my teeth, waited, becoming more impatient by the second.

"Dr. Metzger's office was broken into over the weekend," he said, tapping his hat against his thigh.

My mouth fell open. For a quick second, I was relieved that I wasn't getting dumped, but pushed that aside. Dr. Metzger was the woman I job-shared for and worked in her office on Thursdays and Fridays. This wasn't something I expected. At all.

"Did they steal the television in the waiting room?" I frowned, wondering why anyone would want it that badly. The practice was in an old house right downtown that had been converted into a doctor's office back in the eighties.

Liam shook his head. "No. The exam rooms were tossed, and we think they were searching for drugs."

"Drugs," I repeated. Dr. Metzger was a general

practitioner, meaning she handled everything from sore throats to pregnancy to broken bones. "She might have a few samples from drug reps, but that's it. She fills out prescriptions on the computer and sends them right to the pharmacy and patients have to go pick them up."

"Whoever broke in didn't know that," he replied, rubbing his free hand over the back of his neck.

"Should I call her? I can go in after my shift and help clean up."

Liam stepped close and put his hand on my arm. "Jill, the person who broke in used your code to disable the alarm. That's why no one knew about the break in until they opened this morning."

"*My* alarm code?" I stared at the star on Liam's chest as I worked through it all. I usually arrived early before Dr. Metzger to set up exam rooms or closed for her if she had an emergency, so she'd given me my own access. Everyone who worked there had their own. "They had to get through the locked door, and I always have my keys with me."

He nodded, tilted his head a little. "They went in through a window. Smashed it and then had the thirty seconds to enter the alarm code before the police were called."

"Who would do—" I cut off my own question because I knew the answer. I whipped my head up and looked at Liam. Gone was the look of a lover, the heated gaze and even the playful gleam I'd seen all weekend. Before me wasn't Liam, my lover, but Sheriff Hogan. "Tommy."

He gave a slight nod. "That's what I think."

I closed my eyes and thought about my brother. Not the cute boy I remembered, but the fuck-up I knew now. Turning, I paced the small room. There wasn't much space to walk around as a table and chairs were in the middle where we ate our meals during our breaks.

I rubbed my hands over my face, and wanted to scream in frustration. "When I get my hands on him, I'm going to—"

"You don't want to finish that sentence in front of the sheriff."

I turned to face him and knew, but I wanted to ask anyway. "Is that who you are right now, the sheriff?"

He sighed. "I have to bring you to the station for questioning."

I froze. "Me? I didn't do this." I put my hand to my chest. "I was with you all weekend!"

It wasn't like I didn't have a good alibi, being in bed with the sheriff himself.

"Of course, you didn't," he replied quickly. "I was with you at the pawnshop on Saturday, know your brother's desperate."

I was mad and hurt by Tommy. Again. This time, he'd gone too far. He might steal money, hock things that I needed or wanted to keep because they were sentimental, but messing with my job like that? It was my livelihood. *Our* livelihood since it kept our house. He might not live in it much anymore, but he definitely came to it. I might not see him, but he used the old washer and dryer, ate the food in the fridge. Food *I* bought with money earned working the job he'd just fucked with.

"That's the only reason why you believe me?" I asked, suddenly riled. "That I was in bed with you all weekend and that you were there as I cleaned up Tommy's mess?"

Liam's jaw clenched. "Lash out at me all you want, but you know that's not what I meant. I believe in you. *Know* this wasn't you."

He reached out, stroked a knuckle down my cheek. The gentle gesture soothed me and made me feel guilty.

"I'm sorry," I whispered.

"You have to come with me, baby. Barbara's pulling someone in from a different floor to cover for you."

I felt my cheeks heat with shame at having my family problems exposed to my boss. I'd kept Tommy and my home life separate from work. I showed up on time, did my job, got paid and chipped away at the bills. Except for now. Glancing at the clock on the wall, I saw I would only get four hours pay today.

"Does Barbara think I did it? That I helped Tommy? I work in a hospital and handle drugs as part of my job. They could fire me over this."

I wasn't angry any longer. I was freaked out. This was the only hospital in the county. There were only a handful of doctors in town. While nursing was an in-demand job, there were only so many positions in a town the size of Raines. I didn't want to commute the long way to Bozeman or even Helena. God, this was a mess!

"I have to call Dr. Metzger," I added.

"Now's not the time," Liam said in his calm voice.

"She probably wants to fire me for this!" I hissed, not wanting to shout, for who knew who was walking down the hall.

Liam looked grim. "Dr. Metzger doesn't want you back until this is resolved. She doesn't think you did it, but it *was* your code. I'm guessing you didn't share it with Tommy."

"I don't even *see* Tommy. But the code's my mother's birthday, the same code I use for unlocking my phone, my ATM pin."

Liam offered a small sigh, and I rolled my eyes. A bit of shame at my irresponsibility burned my gut.

"I know, I should come up with something harder, but who would want in my phone? And getting into my bank account? I have less than two hundred dollars in there. Until now, I didn't think it mattered about the alarm at the doctor's office."

My stomach dropped and tears burned the back of my eyes. I might be cleared of the break in, surely Liam would vouch I wasn't involved, but Tommy was. I had no doubt. He would always be my brother, and there would always be another chance of him doing something just like this. I wasn't a reliable employee. Dr. Metzger couldn't trust me with alarm codes or anything now. I didn't know how big the mess was, but her business was built on trust and I'd ruined that. No doubt everyone in town knew of the break in by now.

"I'm calling Tommy."

I went over to my locker, opened it and pulled my cell from my purse. There was a voicemail. I listened to my brother's voice, then hit the button to repeat it, set the phone on speaker so Liam could hear.

"I'm sorry, sis," Tommy said through the phone, his voice unusually tense. "I'm in trouble. I need to pay them back or they're going to fucking hurt me. Why weren't there any fucking drugs in the doctor's office? I could be in the clear now. Find me ten grand, Jilly. I know you're putting money in a savings account for an emergency fund. *This* is an emergency! Shit, I've got to go."

The message ended and I looked up at Liam. His jaw was clenched and he ran his hand over the back of his neck. This wasn't just my brother losing money at the casino. Clearly, he'd gotten in over his head with some bad people.

Ten thousand dollars? I didn't know what to think. How could Tommy lose that much money? He'd implicated himself in the break in. The sheriff heard it, knew he did it and why.

"That *emergency fund?*" I said, rolling my eyes. "Like I said, it has about two hundred dollars in it."

Even if I withdrew that money, it wasn't going to help Tommy. I might not be fired yet, but the voicemail proved I would be because Tommy wasn't going anywhere. He'd always be my brother and always turn to me to clean up his messes. To save him. He was clearly desperate. If he'd broken into the doctor's office and found nothing, that meant he was more frantic than ever. What would he do next?

I was out a job, there was no question. Which meant, I couldn't pay the mortgage and all my bills.

10

ORTER

"Hungry?" I asked as we came in my house through the garage.

Liam had called me, given me an update on the clusterfuck. Fortunately, I wasn't due in court today and had been able to hand off my meetings to someone else in the office or have them postponed so I could get Jill from the sheriff department. They'd questioned her, asking her about her brother and who she thought *they* were from the voicemail her brother had left on her phone. Tommy mentioned *they* when he said he owed ten grand. Of course, Jill had no fucking clue who he was talking about.

I'd been thrilled to collect her when Liam was done with her, to bring her here and take care of her. She was subdued now; the questioning hadn't been fun. She hadn't said a word on the ride from the station. Since she didn't have to go back to the hospital for the remainder of her shift, I drove her to my house.

No way in hell was I taking her to hers with her brother out of control. And I wasn't leaving her alone no matter what she said.

She wanted Tommy to be more than the fucking deadbeat he was. Hell, *I* wanted Tommy to be more than a fucking deadbeat for Jill. She deserved a family that loved her and took care of her. She had Liam and I now, and by extension, our extended families, but it wasn't the same.

Tommy was all the family she had left. The Dukes were a big group. My parents lived in Arizona now but we were still close. Auntie Duke and Uncle Duke—such ridiculous names since we were *all* Dukes—lived in town along with my four cousins. I couldn't imagine no weekly family dinners. No game nights. No summer picnics or even that one year we'd formed a bowling team. That had been interesting. Someone always had my back.

Tommy definitely didn't have Jill's. The opposite, in fact. He was using her, treating her like shit and now, most likely, made her lose her job. Even her reputation around town. I was pissed for her. So was Liam.

While he stayed at the station and tried to track down the fucker, I brought Jill home. Home was *my* house. Hopefully, soon enough, it would be *our* house. Liam's, too. He'd moved back to the family ranch when his dad died last year, but it wasn't permanent. We'd agreed once we claimed Jill we'd live here, or buy a new place for all three of us. He and I would have our own bedrooms, but we'd share Jill. She'd spend the night in our beds, taking turns or however we worked it out. Sometimes, like over the weekend, we'd fuck her while the other watched. Other times, one-on-one. And soon, at the same time. So far, the only time we'd really touched her together was when we finger fucked her pussy in the SUV. Soon though, soon, we'd take her at the same time, make her ours in all ways. One of us would claim her pussy, the other her ass.

She would never be lonely or alone again. Like now, she had shit going on and she wouldn't deal with it all by herself. No fucking way.

She just stood there, not sure what to do, so I pulled her in for a hug, leaned down and kissed the top of her head. She was so small, fragile. In this case, emotionally, although she was the strongest person I knew. I wanted to protect her from anything that didn't put a smile on her face. I wanted to take care of her every need.

Starting with food. It was after noon and she had to be hungry. Stepping back, I helped her out of her heavy coat and hung it on a hook in the mud room.

"Not really," she replied to my question about being hungry.

I kissed her forehead again. "All right, sweetness. Go take a bath and relax and I'll make you at least a snack."

Her sad eyes met mine and she nodded.

I nudged her into the family room and toward the master suite. "Go on. There's nothing you can do right now but relax."

There really wasn't. Liam would deal with finding Tommy and also Dr. Metzger. From what he'd told me, she'd already filled out a police report. Nothing had been stolen since they hadn't found the drugs it was assumed they were looking for. The office only needed glass replaced in one window and a thorough clean up. She'd be back to seeing patients soon enough. She didn't mention that Jill was fired, but being smart, she was waiting to hear how the investigation went.

Tommy was as big a dick as ever, and Jill taking a bath and a nap wasn't going to change that.

Five minutes later, I carried a plate with a ham and cheese sandwich and chips into the bedroom. Based on the sound of the running water, Jill had chosen a shower instead of a bath. It was the quiet sobs that had me swearing under my breath, ditching the snack and opening the bathroom door. Even with the glass shower enclosure fogged with steam, I could see her small form on the tile floor, curled up in a ball.

Quickly stripping, I joined her. Thankfully, she wasn't in the bath because there was no way I could fit in the tub with her, but my shower stall was meant for two. It gave a huge guy like me plenty of space, but still left lots of room for another.

There, with the hot water raining down on her, her head leaning on her bent knees, she cried. Her dark hair clung to her back. My heart wrenched at the sight.

"Sweetness," I said, scooping her up and settling on the bench seat with her in my lap.

She cried against my chest as I stroked my hand up and down her bare, wet back. My dick stirred by her hip, but I ignored it.

"What am I going to do?" she said, her words all gaspy and snuffly from her tears. "Dr. Metzger's going to fire me for this."

"You didn't break into her office," I countered.

"Tommy did. I can't be trusted because of him."

She was partially right. The doctor did have a moral obligation to offer a safe and trusting place for her patients. But she also had a moral obligation to recognize Jill was not Tommy, nor was she responsible for his actions.

I told Jill that.

"He's my brother," she replied.

I gave her a slight squeeze. "Tommy is twenty years old. A man. Should he be responsible for *your* actions?"

"Of course not," she replied right away.

"What about me? You think I should be worried about being with you?"

She shifted so she could look up at me. Her eyes were red-rimmed, but the tears had stopped. "You should. You're the DA. Shouldn't you be worried?"

"If anyone has issue with the woman in my life, that's their problem, not mine. They can go fuck themselves."

That made her smile.

"There's my girl." I leaned down and gave her a soft kiss. "Let's get you all washed up, then you can have that snack I made for you and a nap."

"I'm not a little girl," she grumbled, but without any real oomph behind it.

I looked down her body, took in the soft swells of her breasts with their plump pink tips, the curve of her hips, the fullness of her ass against my thighs. I remembered every single thing we did together over the weekend, thought of all the ways I'd yet to have her. "No, you're not. And I'm seeing after my woman, not treating you like a child."

I stood easily with her in my arms until we were back under the spray. I lowered her feet to the tile and grabbed the soap from the built-in shelf. I began to lather her soft skin and paid special attention to her breasts. While ample, they were so small in my big hands. Soft where I was hard. Smooth where I was rough. Gorgeous. Every single inch of her. "See, I'm not treating you like a child at all."

Her hands settled on my chest and she looked up at me. I saw heat, eagerness. Surprise, as if I was able to arouse her, even after being so upset. With my touch, I could make her forget, at least for a little while. *That* was the goal. There was nothing we could do until we heard from Liam. I'd give her so much pleasure she couldn't remember her own name.

My dick was fully hard now and pointed straight at her belly and when she looked down, she slid her hand around the base. Oh fuck, that felt good. My hips thrust on their own toward her, ready to sink into her tight pussy.

Quickly, before I forgot my own name or came in thick spurts all over her belly, I took hold of her wrist and moved it away. "This is all about you, sweetness. Turn around," I murmured and she did so without comment.

Shit, her ass was gorgeous, all heart-shaped and I wanted to grab hold. So I did, then rubbed my hands along the full curves, ensuring every inch of it was clean.

"Porter." My name was soft and breathless, no longer weepy.

"What, sweetness?"

"I like when you take a shower with me."

One hand reached around her small body and cupped a breast, the other slid between her thighs, covering every nook and cranny with soap, but careful to rinse it all off before I slipped a finger into her.

"I like taking a shower with you, too." She was hot and wet and she clenched down.

"Porter!" she repeated as the palm of my hand pressed against her clit.

Leaning forward, I nipped the spot where her shoulder met her neck. My dick was nestled against her back.

"All clean?" I asked, licking the water from her skin.

She nodded and her head fell back against my chest as I continued to play.

"Yes."

"Good, then it's time to get you all dirty again."

I reached out and shut off the water, opened the door and

grabbed a towel. When Jill stepped out, I carefully dried her by dropping down onto one knee on the thick bathmat so I was at a better height. Perhaps she caught on that I had every intention of doing this myself even though I knew she could do it herself because she said nothing. It was hard to miss when her tits rose and fell with her quick breathing, those gorgeous nipples hard little points. When I dried her pussy, she gasped, obviously sensitive to the soft rasp of the towel. I loved the way her clit was exposed for me to see and know it was a hard nub.

I stood, grabbed a second towel and dried myself with efficient and quick motions, tossed it onto the vanity before scooping Jill up and carrying her to bed. With a rough tug, the blanket and top sheet were on the floor.

Jill laughed. "You're eager," she commented when I had her just where I wanted—naked and in the center of my bed. Her dark eyes were on my dick, which of course bobbed toward her as if it were responding to her words.

I didn't wait, but moved so I was between her parted thighs and my mouth right over her center.

"Porter," she said, realizing my intention.

Looking up her gorgeous, naked body, I met her gaze. Grinned. Oh yeah, I had her exactly where I wanted her. She was already wet for me, the scent of her pussy filling my nostrils. Her skin was warm and damp, dewy even. Lifting one leg, then the other over my shoulders, I cupped her ass, took in the wet folds already parted and ready for me. We'd been at her so much all weekend long, I had to wonder if some of our cum was still deep inside. For some reason, knowing she was marked by us made me feel like a fucking hero. Virile, like I wanted to pound my chest with my fists. My mouth watered in anticipation of tasting her. I loved her pussy and I could eat it for hours. Maybe I would.

We had all afternoon, and I was going to make the most of it. She came for me and Liam as we ate her out before. I loved that she was so responsive, so sensitive to what we did to her. It was like winning a gold medal when she writhed and screamed my name as she came.

"Don't be shy, sweetness. Come as often as you want."

ILL

I FOLLOWED the scent of garlic and something Italian toward the kitchen. After three Porter-induced orgasms from just his mouth and fingers, I conked out when he climbed in bed beside me—fully clothed—and pulled me into his arms. I'd slept hard and didn't even stir when he'd, at some point, climbed from the bed. My scrubs were all the clothes I had, so I put on one of Porter's flannel shirts... my knee-high socks so my feet stayed warm, and nothing else. My hair was a wild mess since I'd never combed it out after the shower, then falling asleep with it wet. I was rolling up the sleeves when I entered the kitchen.

Porter stood in front of the stove, stirring something in a big pot. He was in different clothes than what he'd worn to work this morning. There was over a foot of snow on the ground, and he was barefoot in a pair of well-worn jeans and just a t-shirt. Porter cooking was quite the sight, and it wasn't the delicious scents that made my mouth water.

He looked to me and smiled. "There's my girl." His gaze heated as he took in every inch of me. He came over, took over fixing the sleeves. "I like you in my shirt."

All of a sudden, I felt shy. Earlier, he'd settled between my thighs and had been ravenous, as if my pussy was his only source of sustenance. He'd been insatiable even, and hadn't done anything about his own pleasure. I glanced at the front of his pants. There was a thick bulge—my pussy clenched remembering exactly how big he was—and I had to wonder...

"You never... I mean, don't you need to—"

He lifted my chin with two fingers and I met his eyes. "Say it, sweetness."

"Don't you need to come, too?"

He grinned. "It was all about you earlier."

"And now?" I questioned.

"I licked your pussy so you want to suck my dick?"

I blushed, thinking about kneeling before him, taking his dick as deep as I could into my mouth. He was huge and after spending the weekend together, I hadn't done more than lick the pre-cum from the tip. He'd kept me occupied pleasing him in other ways. I still wasn't sure if I could take him all in my mouth, even if I gripped the base. But I wanted to try, wanted to feel his hands tangle in my hair and pull me closer. I wanted to hear his sounds of pleasure, to feel the power knowing I did it to him.

"Mmm, keep thinking those thoughts, sweetness."

I frowned. "How do you know what I'm thinking?"

He grinned and slid a knuckle over my jaw. "Besides the

flush on your cheeks, your eyes get all foggy and your breathing picks up when you're aroused. Besides, your nipples are poking against my shirt."

I glanced down. Traitorous nipples!

"You want to suck me off, my dick's all yours. Anytime. But right now I want to know how you're feeling."

I shrugged, thought of the mess that was my life, but had no new answers. "Any word from Liam?"

"Only a text that said they have a warrant for your brother's arrest, but haven't found him."

I frowned, wishing things hadn't turned to this for Tommy. At the same time, I was going to have to figure out how to pay my bills without working for Dr. Metzger. "I'm pretty pissed at him at the moment, so he better hide because if I get my hands on him before Liam does—"

"Easy, tiger." He pulled me in for a hug, and I felt a kiss pressed to the top of my head. Against my belly, I felt his dick, long and thick and it pulsed, swelled. "You don't have to worry about your bills, your mortgage. Liam and I are here to help."

The front door opened and closed followed by the sound of boots hitting the floor. Liam was here, but I didn't pay him much thought. No, all my thoughts were on Porter's words. *You don't have to worry about your bills, your mortgage.* Yeah, right!

I pulled back, paced the large kitchen. All the rooms were supersized, perhaps planned that way by Porter since he was so big. Circling the large island, I turned and faced him. "You can't pay my bills for me."

I placed my palms on the cool granite as Liam came into the room. He came around and kissed me on the head.

"Before you ask, Tommy hasn't been found," he said.

"There's nothing new. He's probably hunkered down somewhere."

I nodded, thankful he'd told me right away.

Porter kept his gaze on me even as he crossed his arms. "You don't need to kill yourself working two jobs when you have two men to help with things now." Clearly, he didn't want to talk about Tommy and was like a dog with a dang bone.

I pushed Liam away and narrowed my eyes at Porter. "Men? You think me having you and Liam in my life now is going to solve my student loan debt? That's not how it works."

"It is if you move in here and we pay them for you."

My mouth fell open and I stared at him, then Liam, who still said nothing on the subject, which meant he was in complete agreement, or he knew how to save his own hide. "You don't get it!" I all but shouted.

Porter moved and leaned against the counter on his side of the island. "Explain it to me then."

"To us," Liam finally said. "I want to know the answer to this, too."

I put my hand on my chest. "I give up my house, one of my jobs and I become beholden to you. *Both* of you."

Porter's eyes narrowed. "You're our woman, you're not beholden to us," he countered.

I looked at the ceiling, the recessed lights bright. "You're setting me up to fail! If I rely on you, then what happens when you leave?"

Liam stilled. Porter was quiet for a moment, then he spoke, but his voice was low, almost a whisper. "I'm not your father, and I'm not going to bail. I'm not Tommy and won't use you. While I didn't put a ring on your finger the other night, I vowed before I fucked you bare that this was forever. I have no intention of leaving, but you seem to think this is temporary."

I bit my lip, eyed them both. "I want... I want it to be forever, but I'm scared. Men leave. At least they do for me. I can't rely on anyone but myself, especially when it comes to money. I need to be financially independent."

"This"—Porter circled his hand in the air indicating the three of us—"this is all new, but it's real and deep and serious," he added.

"Very fucking serious," Liam concurred.

"I hear what you're saying," Porter continued. "But you have to understand you're with two men who put you first. We don't want you to work two jobs, not because we don't want you to be self-reliant, but because you work too much. We wouldn't be who we are if we let you push yourself so hard if we can make things easier." He sighed. "We open your car door for you."

I nodded.

"You let us because it's the gentlemanly thing to do. Same goes for walking beside you but closest to the street. And carrying grocery bags. We do all of that not because you can't take care of yourself, but because it's the right thing to do. You're our woman, and it's our job to take care of you."

"And our mothers would kick our asses if they heard we behaved otherwise," Liam added. He looked to me. "Who helped me stuff and lick all those envelopes for the mill levy survey?"

"I did," I said. Before election day, the sheriff's department had to send out notices to everyone in a certain mill district about a measure on the ballot. Liam had been tasked with the job, and I'd gone to the station to help him one rainy

Saturday. We'd done that instead of going to lunch and a movie.

"Why did you help?"

I frowned. "Because there were thousands of them and you would have worked all weekend."

The corner of Liam's mouth went up. "Did you help because you thought I couldn't do it?"

"No, of course not." I shook my head. The idea was actually silly. "You needed help."

He came over, tapped the tip of my nose. "Exactly. You're working at Dr. Metzger's office *and* the hospital so you can pay off your debts. No other reason. We want to help you with that, not because you can't do it, but because helping will make it easier for you."

I relaxed, let the anger fade. They were just trying to be nice. Like they said, gentlemanly. Still... "I understand your point, but there's a big difference between money and licking things."

Liam's eyebrows went up. "I've got something you can lick."

I laughed and rolled my eyes, the tension diffused.

"It's all about trust, sweetness," Porter said, coming around the island, stepping close, close enough to settle his hand on my waist. "We've all fallen hard and fast, but we'll work on it."

My heart thudded and I glanced between the two of them. We might have been hot and heavy all weekend, they might have vowed forever, but this was the first time they'd said how they felt about me. "You've fallen for me?"

They stared at me as if I'd grown a second head.

Liam put his hands on his hips, stared at the floor for a minute, then looked at me. "I don't know if I should spank you or fuck you so you know how I feel about you. Woman, I'm *sharing* you because I love you."

"Perhaps spank, then fuck," Porter offered. He tipped up my chin. "We said forever. We claimed you. Fucked you bare. Of course we've fallen for you. I love you, Jillian Murphy."

A feeling of lightness, happiness, elation pumped through my veins and I couldn't help the smile. "Well, I love you, too."

Both men beamed, as if their favorite football team just won the Super Bowl.

"Love is why we want to make things easier, not because we're men," Porter said.

Liam chuckled. "Well, I hope you love us because we're men, otherwise we need to have a talk. I'd say being in love is a good start toward trust, huh?" Liam asked.

"Definitely," Porter added. "You might not trust us merging bank accounts, but you trust us with your body, giving you pleasure. That's far more precious to me. Liam, you should have seen her earlier, naked, legs over my shoulders, writhing as I ate her pussy."

Liam groaned and moved in on my other side.

I could feel my cheeks heat. "I thought a gentleman didn't kiss and tell."

"I share you with Liam," Porter countered. "No one else."

"Like right now," Liam said, his voice dropping deep in what I now thought of as his sexy voice. His finger slid down my neck and across my shoulder, moving the flannel to expose a few inches of my skin. "Two dicks, baby. Right now. Where do you want them?"

Porter brought his finger up to my lips. Tapped. "Here?" He switched directions and worked it down the center of my body, between my breasts, circled my belly button, then moved lower and dipped into my pussy. He groaned, probably feeling how wet I was, and said, "Here?"

I shivered in anticipation of *here* or *here*.

As he continued to slowly finger fuck me, Liam's hand slid up my thigh, lifting the shirt and cupping my bottom, his thumb dipping between my cheeks. He found my back entrance and I gasped. While his touch was gossamer soft, I went up on my tiptoes surprised by the burst of heat and sensation. He was touching me... *there.* "Or here?"

$\mathcal{L}$IAM

Seeing Jill in Porter's shirt had made me stop in the kitchen doorway. The flannel was an obvious sign that Porter had gotten her out of her scrubs. That, combined with her hair mussed and her cheeks flushed was evidence she'd been fucked and fucked well. The feeling in my chest wasn't jealousy, but something else entirely.

Fear.

If Jill could be so well satisfied by Porter, why did she need me?

Irrational feelings, I knew, but they lingered. Even after a weekend where we'd gotten to know each other even more, in bed and out. Friday night, after we'd had our way with her for a few hours, she'd slept in Porter's bed, wrapped in his arms while I took the guest room. Saturday morning, when the sun was just coming up, I'd picked her up, carried her back to my bed and fucked her, kept her well occupied until lunch. Porter had left us alone to play on our own. Saturday night, she slept with me. Well, *sleep* wasn't the right word since I'd stayed between her lush thighs for hours, then she pretty much passed out. On Sunday while watching football, Liam and I had passed Jill back and forth, from his spot in his favorite recliner in front of the big flat screen and to me on the couch, playing. Fucking. She slept with Porter that night before leaving for work this morning. I'd heard his headboard slamming into the wall, her cries of pleasure. Knew she was well taken care of.

Between all of that, Jill didn't play favorites and seemed to want us both equally.

But fucking didn't make everything right, for as I'd hung up my coat and ditched my boots by the front door, I'd heard them having a heated conversation.

Now, knowing she had issues becoming financially dependent, we had to be careful. No way would she continue killing herself with two jobs, but she was prickly as fuck about it. She might not admit it to herself, even after saying she loved us and wanted forever, we'd be living together soon enough. Her house was small, too small for Porter to move around in. Hell, it was tight for me, too. And if... no, when we had kids... it was just too small.

Porter's house would work, plenty of bedrooms and plenty of land. Or someplace else. While the Hogan ranch belonged to me and my brother equally, the main house was his home now. Since there was plenty of acreage, I could build a place of my own easily enough without getting in his way. *Where* we lived with Jill wasn't the issue. It was *when*.

She was protecting her heart. It was obvious. She'd admitted she was scared. Love was fucking scary. But it was worth it.

Jill was worth it.

And the way she responded to us, so passionately and with complete abandon, she was perfect.

I could tell by the way she went up on her toes as my thumb brushed over her tight asshole that I'd surprised her. "Ever had a dick in your ass?" I asked, kissing along her shoulder. She smelled like Porter's soap, but beneath, all sweet, warm Jill.

"No," she breathed, rolling her hips as Porter worked his finger in her pussy, only to have her shifting nudge the tip of my thumb against her tight rosebud a little harder. Her head fell back against my chest, her eyes closed. "But... oh god!"

No doubt she could come from this, from our finger play, but this wasn't what I wanted. It was time to see if she liked a little ass play, because eventually we'd take her together. I dreamed of her being between us and having us in her pussy and ass at the same time. Two men, two dicks at once.

All weekend long, we didn't even mention ass play. There was enough we wanted to do with Jill to leave that out. But now, it was time to see how she liked it... because ass play was something I *really* liked and wanted to do with Jill. Just thinking of getting my dick in that tight hole had me rock hard. I looked to Porter and he nodded.

"But what, sweetness?" he asked.

"No, I haven't been *fucked* in the ass." She licked her lips and I watched her face. "But I prepared myself for both of you."

Porter's hand stilled and I froze. Porter's eyes held the same mix of surprise and confusion as I felt.

"Prepared?" I asked. My dick, which was already hard, now had a zipper mark in it from my jeans. Shit.

Porter slipped his finger from her and she whimpered. Her eyes opened.

She blushed a fiery shade of red. "I told you I wanted both of you all along, but was too afraid to say."

We nodded and watched her fidget.

"Well, I ordered a butt plug set online and used them."

Porter stepped back, crossed his arms over his chest. He looked so serious, as if he were cross examining a witness in the courtroom, but the way his dick bulged in the front of his pants ruined the effect. "Are you telling me you were walking around with a plug in your ass while we were dating?"

"What?" Her eyes were like saucers. "No, of course not. Well, you saw me on the couch."

"You had a plug in your ass then?" I asked. Holy. Fucking. Shit. Our girl had been playing with herself while her ass had been filled?

She shook her head. "I... god, I'm messing this up. Not that time, but other times when I touched myself, in bed, I put one in. To see what it was like."

"Holy shit," I muttered, this time aloud, imagining her on top of her bed, on hands and knees, reaching back and working one deep inside that virgin hole. Our girl was an anal tease. "You liked it, I'm assuming, made yourself come with your ass crammed full, if you did it more than once."

I didn't think it was possible for her to get any redder, but she did. She nodded.

Porter turned on his heel, flipped off the burner on the stove, then called over his shoulder as he left the kitchen. "Meet me in the family room."

I took Jill's hand and I had just pulled her down onto my lap on the couch when Porter returned, placing a bright pink silicone butt plug, still in its packaging, and a small bottle of lubricant beside it.

"I got this to get you ready for us. I was going to wait a little while since we haven't even fucked you together yet."

"He's right," I said, sliding her flannel off her shoulder so I could kiss it. The top swells of her bare breasts were visible. "Porter's fucked you, baby. I've fucked you, but we've never taken you at the same time. Only our fingers in the garage that first night."

We'd never exactly talked about it, but fucking her solo had been to get her used to the idea of a threesome relationship. To fool around, to play and fuck with someone else watching. It was for Porter and me, too. It wasn't like we were used to being with a woman with someone else around. Now, I was comfortable watching as Porter fucked Jill and probably he felt the same way. But this relationship wasn't about exhibitionism, it was about a threesome.

"That changes now," Porter added. He glanced at me, but I didn't have to say a word. We were in sync on this. It was time to claim our girl together. "It's time to get two sets of hands, two mouths, two dicks involved in making you come."

"You're going to fuck my ass... now?" Her words were a breathless squeak, as if she was equally excited and afraid.

"Do you *want* your ass fucked now?" I asked, held my breath. I'd never taken a woman's ass before. Only played. Fingers, toys, but that was it. If this was what she wanted, hell, I'd happily give it to her because I wanted it, too. "If you have needs, baby, it's our job to take care of them."

"I... I—um..."

I undid the top button of her shirt. The garment being so big, it was all that was keeping it on her shoulders and the flannel pooled about her waist. Leaning her back, I took a nipple into my mouth, sucked until she gasped, until her hands went to my hair.

"How about this, sweetness," Porter said as I switched between one breast and the other. As I played with Jill, he ripped open the toy's package. "We watch you work this pretty pink plug into your ass, then Liam will fuck your pussy while I fuck your mouth. All your holes filled."

She whimpered and writhed in my lap. Oh yeah, she liked the idea. In fact, her pussy juices were getting my pants all wet. Plug filling her now, our cocks soon.

Shit, I was going to come but I wanted to do it in her. I wanted to grip her hips from behind, thrust deep and watch as she licked Porter's dick like a lollipop.

I lifted my head, stood easily with Jill in my arms, then turned to place her on the couch on her knees. I pushed the loose sleeves down her arms so she was free of the shirt, having it settle about her bent knees. She was bare except for some cute socks. "Hands on the back of the couch."

She reached up, did as I said. Porter and I paused, looked our fill. A naked Jill, on her knees facing the back of the couch was an incredible sight.

Porter went around to the other side of the couch so he faced our girl and held up the plug and lube. "We want to watch you put this in, but we'll help if you want that instead. Your choice, sweetness."

Her head was tilted back to meet Porter's eyes. She licked her lips. "I... I want help with the lube, getting all slick. Then I can put it in."

Porter held the lube out to me and I took it, flipped open the lid. Holding the small bottle over the very base of her spine, I let some drizzle down into her crack.

"Spread your legs a little wider," I told her and she complied.

I couldn't miss her wet pussy and above, the tight ring that was now covered in lube. Gently pressing the tip of one finger to her virgin entrance, I swirled the lube around, then began to press in. While she'd played here before, she'd done it solo.

This was the first time she'd had someone touch her like this, so I had to be careful. She'd liked it and that had made her interested in doing it with us... hell, she'd made herself come thinking of us as she had a plug in nice and snug.

But getting a guy involved... or two guys, was different. I didn't want to push her in the wrong direction. Only pleasure for Jill.

I saw her fingers tighten on the back of the couch, but she thrust her ass back toward me and I slid inside. She gasped, her head falling back as she clenched around me instinctively.

"That's it, baby. Such a good girl." I squeezed more lube onto my finger, worked it into her. I'd coat the plug thoroughly, but this was to wake up all those nerve endings I knew were now making her wiggle and squirm, making her nipples tight little peaks.

Porter handed me the plug and I slipped from her to cover it with the glistening lubricant.

With my free hand, I slid my fingers down her spine in a gentle caress, then cupped her ass. "Doing okay, baby?" I asked, my voice soft.

"Yes. I'm ready," she breathed.

Porter stood before her, quiet, eyes on what I was doing. Waiting. No doubt he wanted in her mouth, just as much as I wanted in her pussy. But we'd wait.

It was all about Jill.

Using my thumb, I parted her ass cheek a bit to expose that tight hole. Both of us watched as she reached back, took the toy from me and pressed the soft silicone plug against her entrance, slowly working it in. Holy shit, that was fucking hot. Porter leaned forward and talked with her as she worked it in. He praised her, how gorgeous she was, how proud he was of her taking both of us, telling her men what she liked, what she needed.

At first, it looked as if her body resisted, but she exhaled and it slid right in. She gasped and her eyes widened. I brought my hand down on her upturned ass, giving her a light spank.

She looked over her shoulder at me, then grinned. Oh yeah, the plug was small, but she put it in easily. I had to wonder what size she'd used on herself. She'd be ready for a bigger one, or even our dicks, the next time.

"Ready for more?" I asked, tugging off my shirt, then opening my jeans. There was no time to take off anything else. She'd nodded and wiggled her ass in invitation.

Porter opened his pants, pulled out his cock, stroked it.

"Open up, sweetness. I'll grip the base so you don't take too much."

He was big. *Really* big. Getting in Jill's throat would feel like heaven, but not if it was too much. We might be getting in three of her holes, but this wasn't porn.

Porter stepped close and Jill leaned forward, licked the head of his dick.

He groaned, stroked her hair as she began to play.

While it was so fucking hot seeing Jill suck Porter's cock, my own cock was ready to play too.

The couch was the perfect height for this, elevating Jill enough so she was at the right height to suck Porter. I could stand right behind her and slide right into her pussy.

With the flange of the pink plug parting her cheeks and her pussy all dark pink and glistening, she was stunning. And sexy as hell. My balls ached to fill her up.

Moving close, I put a hand on her hip as I held my dick and coated the tip with all her sticky honey. I glanced at

Porter, who nodded, stilling his motions to shallowly fuck her mouth.

In one slow thrust, I filled her all the way. The entry shifted her forward and she took Porter in to where he had his hand wrapped. She moaned and Porter hissed and shut his eyes.

"Fuck, sweetness, those vibrations are going to make me come."

She did it again as she looked up at him. With her mouth full, she couldn't smile, but I knew she was almost teasing him. I gave her ass another swat, pulled back and plunged deep.

This time, the sound that escaped her hadn't been intentional. She felt too good. Tight, hot, and she fit around me like a glove. I wasn't going to last. Seeing her like this, taking both her men at the same time, was hotter than I'd ever imagined. And the plug in her ass… it was my turn to groan.

We had all night and so this would be a warmup. We'd get her between us in bed and keep on going. Finding her clit, I circled it with my thumb as I fucked her with the drive and need to come. I was losing my focus as my orgasm drew up my balls.

"Your mouth's too good, sweetness. I'm going to come," Porter warned, so she could be ready to swallow.

He came on a harsh growl and I watched Jill's throat work as she swallowed… and swallowed.

When his balls were empty, he pulled from her mouth and stroked back her hair. Now I could hear her scream when she came. I intensified my play on her clit as I fucked her. Hard, deep, our bodies slapping together.

Her inner walls rippled and clenched around me as she came, her head tossed back, her long hair a cascade over her bare back. She cried out, her body almost shaking with the intensity of her release. I tapped the base of the plug, and she clenched even tighter. It was as if she were pulling me into her pussy even deeper, milking the cum from my balls. I couldn't hold back a second longer. Slapping my hand down on the back of the couch, I pressed my body over hers, held myself as deep inside her as I could go and gave over.

The pleasure had black dots dance before my eyes, my breath catch, my muscles go rigid. I was lost in Jill and I never wanted to be found.

13

$\mathcal{J}$ILL

I HELD off my BFF Parker Drew as long as I could. Porter had too, but they worked together and it had been like shooting fish in a barrel for her. From what she'd told me, she'd cornered him in the office and told him—*told him*—we were having a girls' night tonight. He and Liam could pick me up at Cassidy's when we were done, but not a second sooner.

Clearly, she wanted the 411 and wouldn't be delayed any longer. She knew we were together. Knew I'd spent the entire weekend with them. She knew Tommy had broken into Dr. Metzger's office. Hell, everyone in town probably knew both those things.

But she wanted every single dirty detail. And I wasn't talking about Tommy. So after my shift in the recovery room —since I had been cleared of any wrongdoing in the break in, the hospital had no reason to fire me—I drove home, showered and changed and met Parker at Cassidy's. Being Tuesday, it wasn't very busy, only a small dinner crowd and a few who were there for happy hour. I found her in a booth in the back with Ava and Kaitlyn, the two other women who'd also claimed a Duke man and another. It appeared to be a Duke women get-together and since I was with Porter, I was in the club.

"Spill," Parker said as I took off my coat and hung it on the hook on the side of the booth with the others.

I laughed. "At least let me sit down first."

I slid in beside her and said hi to Kaitlyn and Ava. I knew Kaitlyn from elementary school, but she'd moved away when I was perhaps in ninth grade. Her father had hurt Mr. and Mrs. Duke—Porter's aunt and uncle, not his parents—when we were little. He'd died a few years ago and she'd chosen to move back to Raines from where she'd grown up with her aunt in California. She was the town librarian and was dating Duke and Jed. *Dating* wasn't the right word since they were living together and were hot and heavy.

Ava lived with Tucker and Colton on the Duke ranch, and I'd heard that Parker's mom now worked for her at the Feed and Seed.

Parker pushed a beer in front of me. "You're sitting, you've got a drink, now talk."

I couldn't help but grin. "What do you want to know exactly?"

"Are they good?" Parker asked, waggling her eyebrows.

"Of course they're good," Kaitlyn replied, pushing her glasses up her nose.

"We want to know *how* good," Ava clarified.

I blushed. I could feel it. "Well, they're *really* good."

All three of them groaned and Parker slid my pint glass back in front of her. "No talk, no beer."

"Fine, fine! Let's just say two months of just kissing was the longest foreplay ever." Parker pushed the glass back my way, and I took a sip before she could take it away again. "Let me ask you guys…"

They were staring at me intently. I leaned forward and they followed, our heads close over the table.

"When you first had sex," I said, my voice above a whisper to be heard over the music, but not at the next table. "Did you do it together?" I swirled the condensation on my glass. "As in *together* together?"

Kaitlyn and Ava across from me were thoughtful for a moment. "For me, yes. Well, sort of yes. The first night we met, we didn't exactly have sex because I learned who Duke was before we got that far." She swiped her hand through the air. "That's another story for another night. But they did touch me together. Made me come."

"So it wasn't one of them getting you off while the other watched," I replied.

She shook her head. "Oh no, they both get credit for doing that."

"Kaitlyn was talking about the first time they fooled around. The first time I had sex with Colton and Tucker, they took turns. Colton went first, but Tucker was watching, then had his turn." She grinned. "In the kitchen."

Parker and Kaitlyn laughed and had heads turning our way. I was thinking about Sunday afternoon and Parker lifting me up and placing me on the kitchen island, settling himself between my parted legs and fucking me. The size difference between us didn't matter at that height. In fact, he slid right into me without even having to bend his knees.

We looked to Parker next. "The first time? They were all in on it."

I blinked. "You fucked three men at once the first time?" I whispered.

She grinned, rolled her eyes. "That's your question? Then no. Kemp fucked me first with Gus and Poe holding me open for him. They were all involved, but it wasn't like I had three holes filled at once."

Kaitlyn fanned herself while I felt my cheeks get hotter. Parker had no issue with oversharing.

"Did you?" Kaitlyn asked. "Is that why you're asking, Jill?"

I shook my head. "They were on me all weekend, but it was one at a time. Like, Porter would watch me with Liam and vice versa. Or they'd have me alone. But never at the same time until last night. I just wanted to make sure that was normal."

Parker patted my shoulder. "Normal? If you want normal, you need to go date some guy besides a Duke."

Kaitlyn and Ava nodded, tapped their glasses—Ava's filled with beer, Kaitlyn's with iced tea—together in agreement.

"They adore you, Jill," Ava said, reaching out and putting her hand on top of mine. "Seriously, they've been panting after you for months."

"Months," Kaitlyn repeated, nodding.

"I love them, too," I admitted.

"What is it then?" Parker asked. "Too bossy?"

"Dominant?" Ava added.

"Alpha?" Kaitlyn threw out there.

"All of the above."

"Again, totally a Duke thing. But they love you and want to take care of you and have made you the center of their world."

I gave a slight shrug, but thought of the way Porter constantly checked on me, if not verbally, at least with his eyes. They catered to my every whim—not because I was an invalid or a child—because they wanted to see me smile. They made me come first. Every time. They opened doors for me, helped me with my seat belt. Made sure I'd eaten.

And they *could* be bossy.

"I have baggage," I admitted. "You heard what my brother did."

They nodded. Yeah, just as I thought. The whole town must know.

"My father drove drunk and almost killed Mr. and Mrs. Duke. Talk about baggage," Kaitlyn admitted. "I'm not my father and you're not Tommy."

That was a good point. What her father did... god, it had been horrible and he'd gone to jail. I didn't blame Kaitlyn for it. I got her point. Tommy's mess was just that, Tommy's mess.

I sighed, thought of Porter and Liam. My heart stuttered, but I smiled. "I love them."

All three women cheered as if a group of people suddenly rushed over with a bunch of balloons and a huge Publisher's Clearing House check. I couldn't help but grin as Ava showed us her ring and we moved on to talking about possible summer wedding dates. Since I had to be at the hospital first thing in the morning, we made it an early night. We texted our men letting them know we were all done. I decided to go to the ladies' room before we left. In the back hallway, there was a man leaning against the wall. He stepped into my path and I stopped, suddenly nervous. He wasn't as big as Liam, but he was solid. He wore a baseball cap low over his face, a big black jacket and dark jeans. It was his eyes though. No warmth in their depths that had me taking a step back.

I saw movement out of the corner of my eye and realized another man had come up behind me. He was short, but built like a barrel. His nose had been broken a few times and never fixed. He grinned and not in a kind way.

"Easy, Jill Murphy," the guy in front of me said. I spun back to stare at him, wide-eyed and petrified. "We're not going to hurt you. We just want to talk about Tommy."

My stomach jumped into my throat. Oh god. Who were these men? What had they done with Tommy?

I turned so my back was to the wall instead of one of the men. The bathrooms were to the right, the main restaurant area to the left, but the men blocked both. While I could hear the music from the jukebox and knew people were out there, no one was nearby.

"What do you want?" I said. I could scream, but I wasn't sure what they'd do. Did they have guns tucked away in their coats? Knives? As long as they didn't drag me out the back door, I was safe. *Safe-ish.*

"Your brother owes us some money." The guy's lips were chapped and he hadn't shaved in a few days. Strange, the things you noticed when you were freaking out.

"I don't have any money," I replied. "My car's over fifteen years old. I work two jobs."

"That's right," he replied. "Two jobs. Two places to get drugs to pay off his debt."

"You mean the hospital?" I asked. I shook my head. "Drugs are kept in these big machines with codes and scanners."

"A little at a time from your patients. You've got pockets."

"I work in recovery!" I countered. "Everyone's just come from surgery with IVs. There aren't any pills."

"Morphine works. I'm sure you can find some Oxy."

I shook my head. "I can't. It's impossible. Maybe a pill here and there, but that's it."

They grinned and nodded. "You can. Your brother went

into hiding and hasn't been able to pay, so you will." They stepped closer. Loomed. I swallowed down my fear. "If not the hospital, then go back to your doctor."

It seemed the one guy was the leader, the other just backup because he hadn't said a word. "Get on her computer and send prescriptions to the pharmacy for fake patients for us to pick up."

"That's illegal."

Duh. God, that was a dumb thing to say. Of course it was illegal. These were bad men who didn't give a shit about the law.

"For you." Oh god, I was the one who was going to get caught, not them. They weren't getting their hands dirty at all. "But you're fucking the sheriff and the DA, right? They won't arrest you if they're getting pussy. Do this or your brother's going to be found piece by piece across the county. Tell them about our little chat and you'll both be found by the wolves."

I gulped. No wonder Tommy had been so frantic to get into Dr. Metzger's office.

"This is our little secret, right? Tell your men and we kill your brother, then you." He patted my shoulder and they walked off together. "We'll be in touch."

 ILL

I SAGGED against the wall as my heart was beating out of my chest.

Oh. My. God.

What was I going to do? I pulled my phone from my purse, pressed Tommy's number with shaky fingers. It went right to voicemail. I hung up, shoved the phone away.

Shit. Shit! A woman came down the hall, smiled at me as she made her way to the bathroom. I realized then I'd been gone for a while. Liam! Oh, shit. He was coming from the station to pick me up.

I took a deep breath, then another as I made my way back through the restaurant. Liam was walking toward me, a big grin on his face. I didn't see the others, so I had to assume they'd already left. God, he looked so good, so handsome in his jeans and heavy coat. He took his hat off when he saw me.

I wanted to wrap my arms around him, have him hug me close, kiss the top of my head. I wanted to hear his heartbeat as I pressed my head to his chest, breathed in his clean scent.

But no. I couldn't let him do that. He was the sheriff! I was going to have to break the law or Tommy would be cut up into little bits. Then there was Porter. It was his job to prosecute criminals, to put them in jail. They were both on the right side of the law. They worked for justice, for keeping the peace. And they were dating a soon-to-be criminal. What was I going to do?

I couldn't tell them the truth. Not yet. Not now. I had to think this through. If I didn't do what those men wanted, they'd kill Tommy. If I did, then I could ruin both their careers.

"Hey, baby." His smile slipped when he got a close look at me. "What's the matter?"

I had to think of something fast, of some excuse as to why I was all freaked out. Miserable. Scared. I was a horrible actress, and there was no way I could fake being all right after that.

"I, I... um, got my period. I've got horrible cramps."

He frowned, but didn't bolt like some guys would have at the mention of girl stuff. Fortunately, it seemed he wasn't knowledgeable enough about an IUD to know I hadn't had a period in years.

"Okay, let's get you home and what? Need some aspirin and a heating pad?"

"Can you just take me home? To *my* house?" I clarified. It was easy to feign miserable cramps when I felt miserable. "I've got everything I need there and I'm not very good company right now."

I wanted to throw the covers of my own bed over my head and think. Hide.

He wrapped an arm around my shoulder and steered me toward the door. "Sure, but I'm staying with you. No way will I leave my girl alone when she's hurting."

I almost started crying then because he was so fucking sweet, but willed it back.

An hour later, I was spooned up against a sleeping Liam in my bed. He hadn't done anything except kiss me sweetly and pull me into his arms. Porter had been called and hoped I felt better, but had said he was glad Liam was with me. Two caring men. They loved me. But they wouldn't soon enough when I broke the law. As I listened to Liam's deep breathing, I stared at the dark walls and wondered what I was going to do.

* * *

I MADE it through my shift at the hospital, thankful the number of scheduled surgeries was small. Both Liam and Porter had texted to check in. It had been easy to reply on a break since the messages were short and easy to fake. Over lunch, I went into one of the emergency stairwells and tried calling Tommy again. To my surprise, he answered.

"Hey, sis."

"Tommy, are you all right?" I asked.

"I'm fine."

"Where are you?"

"What, you want to sic your boyfriends on me?"

I pulled my cell away from my head and stared at it for a few seconds. "No, I thought maybe two guys, one with a crooked nose might have found you."

Now he was quiet. "Do what they say, Jilly."

"Yeah, I figured that out," I muttered. If I knew what they looked like, then that meant I'd talked with them. Tommy didn't even ask if I was all right or be mad because they'd approached me. Threatened me.

"They're going to hurt me if you don't."

If there was a possibility of a brain transplant, it was my brother who had gotten one. Who was this guy talking to me? I didn't hear anything of my little brother in him. "Hurt you? They *threatened* me, Tommy."

"You've got the sheriff and the prosecutor to protect you from jail. Just get the scripts and everything will be fine."

I had to wonder if he'd given them the idea of me writing fake prescriptions.

"For how long? You think they're the kinds of guys who will ever let me stop?"

"Look, sis. I like my fingers attached. What's a few prescriptions?"

"It's my nursing license, Tommy," I snapped. "Not only can I be arrested, but I can lose my career. My livelihood." I paced back and forth across the concrete landing. "Dr. Metzger hasn't even said if I should come in tomorrow. I'm probably fired and that means I can't pay the bills. The mortgage. I could lose the house, Tommy."

"You're fucking two guys who can make it all go away. Smart thinking."

I was stunned and insulted and hurt and pissed.

"You know what? *You* got yourself into this. Why don't *you* get the money? Get a job and earn it. Or leave town. Run. Get away from all the stuff you're involved in."

"Look, Jilly, I've got to go. Talk soon."

The line went dead.

I shoved my cell into my scrub top pocket next to my notepad and pen. I made a funny scream sound that echoed off the concrete walls as I tugged at my hair.

How dare Tommy say that? How dare he call what I had

with Liam and Porter something so... so tawdry? God, he wanted me to risk my career, my relationship, everything just so he didn't have to face the consequences of his mistakes?

But they were going to *kill* him.

And me.

What could I do? Not do what they wanted and just go right on living, watching my back so I wouldn't be grabbed and chopped up into pieces? Tell the guys to fuck off and then they'd kill Tommy? Maybe me, too?

I sat down on a cold step, put my elbows on my knees. I could tell Liam and Porter what was going on, but the men said they'd kill Tommy, and I believed them. No matter how much I hated him right now, I didn't want him dead. I couldn't live with that.

I was screwed. Write fake prescriptions or my brother dies. I die. But a relationship with Liam and Porter was out of the question. I couldn't drag them into this. *Their* careers could be ruined. Their actions would be scrutinized. People would believe they'd been helping me, or at least bending the rules for the woman they loved. Liam would be removed from office. Porter could be disbarred. It wasn't fair to them that they be with me.

Tears filled my eyes and I blinked them back. God, for the first time in my life, I relied on someone else, *two* someones, put hope in a relationship. In love. And, just like with Mom, it was ruined. Of course, she'd had no choice with cancer.

I had a choice now. I had to leave town. Run away. I couldn't do what the men wanted. I couldn't write fake prescriptions, couldn't imagine where the drugs would end up, who would be hooked or hurt by my actions. I couldn't stay in Raines and see Liam and Porter, watch them move on with another woman. If I left, they couldn't hurt me. And if I told Tommy to run, too, then maybe he would listen. Maybe he'd have a chance.

I pulled out my cell, sent a text to him.

ME: *They'll come after you. Run.*

I STOOD, took a deep breath, let it out. Tried to push down the heartache, the pain I felt at having everything, then losing it all. After my shift, I'd go to the ATM, get the two hundred I had in savings, go home, pack my car with whatever would fit and leave.

 ORTER

BY THE TIME I got to the station and sat down across from Tommy Murphy in the interrogation room—it also served as a meeting room since the place was so small—Liam had been grilling him for over an hour.

The resemblance between brother and sister was obvious. Jill and Tommy had the same dark hair, eyes and face shape. But that was where it ended. Tommy was tall, lean-muscled and wiry, where his sister was petite and had soft curves. Jill smiled with her eyes and had deep concern and affection for everyone. She was a giver, a nurturer. And she'd wasted her time and energy on this fucker.

Tommy sneered, his eyes cold. His arms were across his chest as he slouched in his chair, an overly confident posture for one who'd been arrested for breaking and entering with the intent to commit a felony. His hair was long and unruly, greasy, as if he hadn't showered in a few days. He had on a

University of Montana hoodie sweatshirt two sizes too big, a pair of jeans with a rip in the knee and sneakers. When I rested my forearms on the table and stared him down, he didn't even flinch.

Liam was equally relaxed, no doubt acting calm when he wanted to throttle the fucker. But, he had procedure to follow. The sheriff couldn't beat up a suspect, no matter how much he wanted to.

"Let's recap for the DA, shall we?" Liam said.

Tommy rolled his eyes. "Whatever."

"Porter Duke, District Attorney of Raines County has now joined the interview," Liam said in a clear voice for the recording. "Tommy says he was in bed sleeping at the time of the robbery."

Bullshit, especially since Jill had the voicemail with him admitting the crime. "I understand you owe people some money," I said instead.

Tommy shrugged. "You've got a mortgage, right? You owe people some money, too."

"Ten thousand dollars, your sister says," I continued.

"It's all fine. Jilly's helping me out."

I sat and stared at him, my eyebrow raised. "By letting you clean out her house? What else are you going to pawn?"

He picked at a hangnail on his thumb. "It's just meaningless stuff. Electronics, old jewelry. It's not like Jill needs it. She's never home."

Because she works all the time.

"How's she helping you out?" Liam asked.

Besides paying off the remainder of her mom's medical bills all by herself.

For the first time, Tommy looked away. "It's not like she's going to get in trouble. She's fucking the two of you. She got off for the break in, free and clear."

I glanced at Liam.

"She didn't break into Dr. Metzger's office," he said, leaving off the fact that we were her alibi.

Tommy shook his head and said, "Yeah, and even though her alarm code was used, she's still got a job. Nothing happened to her."

I hadn't heard if she got her job back or not. He was too cocky with his sister's life.

"What are you saying, she gave you the code?" I asked. "That she's your accomplice?"

Tommy shrugged, scratched his head. "Like I said, she knew you'd help her out. I mean, I *am* her brother."

I instantly thought of Sierra, the woman who'd had a "relationship" with me to get out of going to prison. It had worked, her case thrown out because of a technicality, which was me fucking her. And that had gotten me fired and I'd had to return to Raines, tail between my legs. I hadn't tried to get serious with a woman after that until Jill.

Jill loved her brother, perhaps too much for how he treated her. But he was all she had. With her mom dying of cancer, her dad bolting when she was a little kid, she craved family. She'd do anything for Tommy. I'd seen the way she resigned herself to retrieving her mom's pin from the pawnbroker, forking over her own cash to get it back. Shit, while I didn't have any siblings, if one of my cousins pulled that shit, I'd have beat the crap out of him. She hadn't cut Tommy off, changed the locks on the house. Stopped giving him cash. She was an enabler, but to what extent?

"What else is Jill doing to get money for you?"

Tommy leaned forward, grinned. "It's pretty tight. I mean, writing fake scripts is a pretty sweet plan, especially getting in with you two with a get-out-of-jail-free card dangling from your dicks."

Holy fuck.

Writing fake prescriptions? That was a worse offense than breaking and entering. And she was getting away with it. Clearly, Dr. Metzger didn't know. Hell, we were fucking her and we didn't know. God, she was good. She switched from dating to fucking just so she could keep herself out of jail. And both of us. The sheriff *and* the DA.

"Don't disrespect your sister by talking about her like that," Liam snarled.

Tommy held up his hands in surrender.

"Whatever, man. Just telling it like I see it. I mean, if I swung the other way, I'd fuck both of you, too."

Liam's fists clenched and I was impressed with his restraint. I was too distracted by what Jill had done to me. *Was* still doing.

"How long's this been going on?" Liam asked, his voice deep, almost a growl.

Tommy shrugged. "Recent. How long you two been banging her?"

"Where's the proof?" Liam asked.

He tipped his chin, indicating the plastic container on the table that had the things from his pockets when he was brought in. "She texted me earlier. Told me to watch out for you."

I handed him the phone and he ran his fingers over it, then dropped it on the table. Liam picked it up, read it, then handed the cell to me.

JILL: They'll come after you. Run.

I GLANCED AT LIAM, his jaw clenched, eyes narrowed. Fuck.

107

Jill had warned Tommy the sheriff's department was closing in? Telling him to flee the cops?

I stood, loomed over Tommy. His dark eyes widened, but he grinned even bigger. I wanted to punch the fucker, but I had to deal with Jill. Liam could get the pleasure of tossing him into a cell.

I'd fallen for it. Again. Jill wasn't so sweet after all. Oh, her pussy tasted like candy, but that wasn't all I wanted from her. I'd hoped for her heart, but all I got was the shaft. At least this time I learned the truth early enough. I could recuse myself. Get one of the ADAs to take her case when she was brought before the judge. Because Jill was going down, and it wasn't to her knees to suck me off.

* * *

JILL

THE CAR WAS PACKED. I filled two beat up suitcases with clothes and things I'd need wherever I settled. The cash from the ATM along with my credit cards would have to hold me over until I found a job. I'd head south, no sense staying in cold any longer than I had to. Arizona, maybe. It wouldn't be snowing outside like it was here. The wind rattled the shutters and I knew we'd have inches overnight. Time to hit the road before it got even worse.

I set the thermostat down and ate whatever random bits of food were left in the fridge for dinner. I was tugging on my coat when the doorbell rang. After the awful men cornered me at Cassidy's, I was beyond nervous. When I saw it was Porter through the peephole, I was relieved. Well, relieved I wasn't going to be killed. But I didn't want to see him. How was I going to say goodbye? How was I going to tell him I loved him too much to be with him? My heart actually hurt as I opened the door.

He stepped in and I closed the door behind him, a few flakes following.

"Hi," I said lamely.

"When were you going to tell us, Jill?" Porter asked.

I stared at him wide eyed. He knew I was leaving?

"Um, well, I…"

"You weren't going to, were you?" He sounded angry. He *looked* angry. There was no tender smile, eyes that held love, heat.

Now, he was tense. Hard. Cold, and not from the growing storm outside.

I shook my head.

"I thought you were The One." He ran his hand through his damp hair, the snow that had collected on the walk from his SUV having melted. "Fuck, was I wrong. I fell for it. I fell for *you.*"

Tears filled my eyes at his harsh words. It was better he be mad. It would be easier for him to move on if he hated me. I hadn't done anything wrong… yet. But that didn't matter.

"I'm sorry," I replied meekly.

"No, you're not. You're on your own. No, you've got Tommy. Don't come to me when the shit hits the fan, sweetness. Because it will."

With that he tugged open the door and left. I watched as he stormed down my walk and climbed into his huge SUV and drove away.

I closed the door, leaned against it and slid down to the floor and cried.

Porter hated me. Liam probably did, too. Tommy was never going to turn his life around. I just had to hope he was arrested before the men from Cassidy's caught up with him. I'd warned him to get out of town. I just had to hope he listened. I couldn't be responsible anymore. I had to take care of myself, just like I always had. I picked myself up, grabbed my coat, my keys, climbed in my car. I was all alone. As I drove out of town toward Clayton and the interstate, I realized I'd only really been with Liam and Porter for five days, so not much had changed. I was exactly the same, except for one thing.

A broken heart.

$\mathscr{L}$IAM

"Fuck, what a day." I ran my hand over the back of my neck as I opened Porter's fridge and pulled out a beer.

I popped the top and tossed it in the trash under the sink. All I wanted to do was settle on the couch with Jill in my lap and watch a movie. When had I turned into an old fart? Oh yeah, when I fell in love.

"A good one though," I continued. "Tommy's a small fish. We got him, but he gave us two others for a lighter sentence. That kid's a little shit, thinking only of himself. Whatever. I'm off duty, so to make us forget it all, I stopped by the adult store and got our girl a little—well, not so little—jeweled plug. I think she'll look gorgeous with a bright green gem parting her ass cheeks."

My cock went hard just thinking about her on all fours

on Porter's ottoman, ass up, her ass beautifully plugged. I took a long swig. Fuck, that tasted good.

I turned and finally looked at Porter.

He was leaning against the counter, staring out the windows that lined one wall of the great room, although it was too dark out to even see the snow coming down.

"You're too uptight to have been in our girl. Is she in the tub? I want to tell her the latest."

"She's not our girl."

I frowned, looked around. I didn't see Jill, didn't smell her shampoo. Hell, it didn't *feel* like she was even here. It was a little woo woo to even sense that, but I did.

"Where is she?" I asked him straight.

He looked at me and shrugged. "Her house."

"Okay," I said the word slowly, clearly missing something. "Why the fuck is she over there? I can go get her. She shouldn't be driving in this."

He looked me in the eye. "She's at her house because it's over."

"Over," I repeated. Was he drunk? That was the only thing I could think of, even though he didn't even drink.

"She used us." I frowned, and he continued. "She admitted she was writing fake scripts, just like her brother said."

I set my beer on the island with a loud thunk. "What the fuck are you talking about?"

"I went over there. She had no intention of telling us the truth, that she was using us, *fucking* us so that she'd stay out of jail."

That didn't jive with anything I'd learned today. Tommy was a douche canoe who didn't give a shit about his big-hearted sister. As soon as I offered him a sweet deal with barely any jail time, he rolled on those who were pretty much extorting money from him.

"She told you she's been writing fake prescriptions through Dr. Metzger's office?"

He nodded.

"She said those words. She said, *I've been writing fake prescriptions.*"

"No."

I sighed, tried to remain calm, but getting answers out of Porter was like trying to get the truth out of Tommy. "What did she actually say?" I slapped my hand on the granite. "Dude, what were her fucking words?"

He clenched his jaw. "I asked her if she were ever going to tell us and she said no."

I stared at him, trying to work it all out in my head. "We picked up two guys from Clayton, the guys who Tommy owes money. Tommy doesn't have the cash, as you're well aware."

He nodded.

"Tommy couldn't get the cash, so he got the stupid, and desperate, idea of searching for drugs in Dr. Metzger's office. When that didn't pan out, the guys got pissed, put the heat on Tommy. When they learned his sister worked there, they got the idea of the fake prescriptions. A perfect way to get pills. Tommy could sell them and get the cash to pay the guys back."

"A drug dealer. Jesus, Tommy's a little fuck," Porter murmured.

"They threatened Jill," I said, my words sharp. Cutting. When I heard that, when the guy with the busted nose had said that, I'd had to leave the interrogation. I'd had to have a deputy sit with the asshole while I cooled off.

"What do you mean they threatened her?" Porter's voice went deep and deadly.

"Told her she had to get the scripts or they'd kill Tommy. They'd kill *her*."

"What the fuck?" Porter said, spinning on his heel and pacing.

"From what Tommy said, she refused to do it, and he was pissed. You ready for this?"

He stopped looked my way.

"The text Tommy showed us, she wasn't telling Tommy the cops were after him. She was talking about the two fuckers who threatened her."

"She told him to run," Porter added.

I nodded. "Yeah, because she'd decided she wouldn't do what they wanted. Why the fuck did you think she would do something like that?"

"Because she's fucking the sheriff and the DA."

"Jesus, you believed Tommy?"

He shook his head. "I told you what happened back east. I'd been in a relationship and the woman had only been with me to get her off, and I don't mean sexually. She'd been up for tax evasion and other stupid shit and she used me, fucked me so that I could keep her out of jail. Turns out, she stayed out of jail and I got fired. Pretty much got kicked out of working in the state."

"Sienna?" I remembered this story, knew she was why he hadn't dated much. One night stands, but nothing real, not until Jill.

"Sierra," he corrected.

"Sierra's long gone, dude. That was *years* ago. I never met the woman, but Jill's nothing like her."

He sighed. "I know, but between being burned in the past and Tommy's words, I blew it."

My cell rang and I pulled it from my pocket.

"Hey, Parker," I said.

"She's gone."

I glanced at Porter. "Who's gone?"

Porter came around the counter, stood beside me. I lowered my cell, hit the speaker button.

"Jill, you idiot," Parker yelled. "She's gone."

"Where?"

"Gone! She texted and said she was fine but had to leave town."

"Oh shit," Porter murmured. He put his hands on the back of his neck, elbows out and exhaled. "*That's* what she was talking about earlier. She'd already decided to leave and wasn't going to tell us."

"And you thought she was talking about stealing scripts."

"Who's stealing prescriptions?" Parker asked. "Jill wouldn't do that."

"No, she wouldn't," Porter said. "Did she say where she was headed?"

"Arizona. Something about starting over where it was warm. You two need to find her."

Porter was already heading for the garage. "On it," I said, then hung up. "I've got the sheriff SUV. We'll take that."

Porter changed directions and went out the front door. The snow was coming hard and fast but I doubt he even felt it. I was pissed at him for fucking things up with Jill, but I could understand how it had happened. Now he was a man on a mission, because he wasn't raised to let his woman drive alone on a night like this. Hell, spend the night by herself in a strange hotel. To let her spend one minute more thinking we didn't love her.

Jill was out there. Alone. We had to find her and we had to make this right.

 ILL

I WILLED MYSELF TO SLEEP, but it wouldn't come. The sliver of light peeking through the curtain highlighted the square tiles on the ceiling, which I'd counted over and over, like sheep. I was exhausted, having worked all day and then driven fifty miles in a Montana snow storm. By the time I pulled into the parking lot of a chain hotel off the highway, my muscles ached from being so tense. I'd leaned forward like a little old lady as I drove well below the speed limit because of blowing snow. I should've stayed home and headed out in the morning when the front was to clear away. I hadn't been thinking clearly. I hadn't really been thinking at all. That was better than actually listening to the voice in my head.

It had been relatively easy to do with the radio blasting, but now, in the quiet of the hotel room with only the hum of the heater to distract me, I thought of *them*.

I had on sweats, thick socks and a hoodie sweatshirt because while the heat worked in the room, the blanket was thin. I missed Porter's internal furnace. I missed Liam's arms as he held me close through the night. The bed was empty, cold. Even after Mom died, I hadn't really felt this alone.

I'd had Tommy to think about, to take care of. He'd been sixteen at the time and needed a ride to school. Needed dinner on the table after. Needed clean clothes.

Now, he didn't need me. That was obvious. I had to wonder if he even loved me. Did he even know what that meant? To care so desperately for someone you'd do anything for them? To—

There was a knock on the door and I bolted upright. I'd turned the deadbolt, slid that bar thing across. No one was able to get in, even if they had a keycard.

"Jill!"

I jumped from the bed, stared in the darkness at the darker door. Only a tiny circle of light showed through the peephole. Porter?

The knock came again. "Jill, it's Porter and Liam. Open the door."

I blinked and my heart skipped a beat.

"Please," he added.

I raced to the door, slid the bar over, turned the handle.

Before I could take in more than two big men, I was picked up in Porter's arms as he walked into my room. Liam must have flipped on the light as he shut the door. Porter didn't stop until he was on the bed and I was settled on his lap.

"What are you two—"

"Shh," Porter murmured. "Just let me hold you, sweetness. I think I aged ten years worrying about you."

"I'm fine."

"Shh." He wrapped his arms around me tighter and the cold from his shirt and pants seeped into me. I shivered and he rubbed my arm, pulled me in even tighter.

Liam dropped to his knees in front of us, brushed my tangled hair back from my face. His jaw was covered in pale whiskers, his hair stuck up in places. While his blue eyes were tender, I couldn't miss how tense he was. "You okay?"

I nodded against Porter's chest. I could feel his heart beating a mile a minute. He was truly freaked.

"How did you find me?" I asked after a minute.

Liam's mouth turned up at the corner. "I *am* the sheriff." His uniform shirt backed up the words. "The roads are shit, so I requested a snowplow and we followed right behind. Cleared a path for us. We checked every hotel on the way and the front desk was very cooperative with giving your room number."

In this remote part of the highway, there weren't all that many hotels, and only clustered at a few of the exits.

"Why did you leave, baby?"

I couldn't look at Liam for this. It hurt too much.

He tipped my chin up, made me look at him. "I... I couldn't hurt you like that."

Porter groaned. "I hurt *you*, sweetness. I'm so sorry. I didn't mean anything I said. Not one word."

Porter loosened his hold and Liam took me from his lap, moved to sit on the bed so I was on his lap instead. Porter took my hands, rubbed my knuckles. His eyes met mine and I saw anguish there. "A long time ago, I was in a relationship with a woman who got in trouble with the law. I worked at the DA's office and her case came up, but got thrown out because of our relationship."

What? How dare that woman use Porter like that. "It wasn't your fault."

He shrugged. "It was a long, complicated legal mess, but she got away with it, I got fired and pretty much lost all chances of being hired in that town. That's why I moved back home." Sighing, he continued. "Like I said, that was years ago. I let that mess cloud my judgment with you. I jumped to conclusions when I shouldn't have."

"You thought I was with you because of my brother's mess."

He actually blushed and looked away for a moment. "For a little while earlier, yes. It seems you're not the only one with trust issues, sweetness."

The ache that had been lodged in my chest like a knife lessened. They were here, they were holding me and it felt… perfect.

"We apprehended two men from Clayton," Liam said. "One had a hook for a nose."

I stiffened at the mention of the guys from the bar. "Ah, I guess you know who I'm talking about."

"I only met them once. Well, I didn't *meet* them, they approached me at Cassidy's. Threatened me."

Porter's hand tightened around mine.

"The night I picked you up?" Liam asked.

"Yes."

"You didn't have your period, you were upset because of them," he added, putting it all together. "I'm the sheriff and some guys just threatened to kill you. Why didn't you tell me?"

"Sweetness, why didn't you tell us?" Porter repeated, much more calmly than Liam. "What's the point of having two big men like us around if we can't protect you?"

I gave Porter a small smile. "They said they'd kill Tommy. And me, if I told you."

I felt a growl rumble through Liam's chest. "Tommy rolled on them. They talked."

I gasped. "What do you mean? You caught Tommy?"

Porter looked over my head at Liam, then back at me. "You didn't know?"

I shook my head.

"Earlier today. He was holed up at a friend's house. His car was spotted from the road and we arrested him."

I felt… sad that Tommy was in jail, but it was where he belonged.

"Tommy gave information about the guys who *approached* you."

"I wasn't going to do it!" I gripped the front of Liam's uniform shirt. "I couldn't write fake prescriptions. I couldn't mess with Dr. Metzger like that, and I couldn't imagine where the drugs would end up, who'd get hurt. Besides, I'd be too nervous and wouldn't be able to get away with it. I promise. I wouldn't have done it."

Liam put a finger over my lips. "Shh. We know and so does Dr. Metzger. I called her earlier with an update about her case. She said she welcomes you back, but said to take this week off, with pay, to have a well-earned break."

I ducked my head, relieved to still have the job and my relationship with the doctor not in tatters. I knew Liam and Porter didn't want me to work two jobs, but it wasn't about *working* them, but *having* them. I didn't want to lose my job because of Tommy, because of this mess, and perhaps Liam didn't say anything about it since he understood.

"Those assholes, they're why you left?"

I shrugged, then looked up at Liam. "I didn't have much choice. If I stayed, I'd have to do what they wanted. I just… couldn't. Not just for me, but for you."

"For us?" Liam asked, frowning.

"Your jobs. You'd get fired. Just like what happened to you with that woman," I said to Porter. "I didn't want anyone to think less of you because of my mess."

Liam turned me about so my knees settled on the bed on either side of his hips and I faced him. He cupped my face with his big hands.

"It's not your mess. It never was, but it definitely isn't now. You hear?"

I nodded, but couldn't go far with him holding my head.

"I know you love your brother, but he's going to jail. He made a deal and is going to testify against bigger fish, but he's going to do time."

He was studying me, clearly worried about how I was going to react. They knew how much he meant to me, all the things I'd done for him without a bit of gratitude.

"Good."

He frowned.

"Good?" Porter asked.

I bit my lip, then said, "I sent him a text, told him those two guys would be after him and that he should run so he didn't get hurt. I wasn't telling him to avoid the law, just the opposite. Maybe he'd go somewhere new and get a job and abide by the law." Liam looked at Porter, who nodded. "I'm glad you caught him though. He… he needs to go to jail for what he did. I tried my best, but it wasn't good enough. He—"

"Shh," Liam said, kissing my forehead. "You did a great job with him. Just because he's a fuck-up doesn't reflect on you. He was dealt a bad hand with your dad leaving you all and then your mom getting sick, just like you were. You chose to bust your ass for a degree and to work. To care for people. He chose the shortcuts and found out that's not how it works."

He dropped his hands, set them on my thighs.

"You're not alone, sweetness. You have us. Well, you have Liam, and you have me, too, if you'll forgive me."

"I love you. Of course I forgive you."

He grinned and his chest puffed up. *I* made him like that. Happy, relieved. Loved.

"Will you forgive me?" I asked in return.

"You've done nothing wrong."

I felt like we were getting a second chance. I'd been giving my heart and soul to Tommy when he didn't want it. He didn't value it. I *should* have given it to Liam and Porter. They'd proven they would cherish both. They'd proven it time and again and I'd mistaken it for smothering. For being overbearing. Boy, was I wrong. "Remember when we argued about you helping me with money? With working too hard?"

Porter picked up my hand, kissed my palm and nodded.

"You're right. I work too hard. But I also don't want you to take on my debt. That's not fair." I paused and took a moment to feel. There was no doubt. I felt confident in my plan because I had these two men. "I'm going to sell the house. I was saving it because of Tommy; it was the one place that connected us to Mom. To what I longed to get back. That was the past and... and you two are the future. The house sale will pay off all my bills and I'll have some left over. I'm going to go back to school. Dr. Metzger and I talked about me being a nurse practitioner, well, before all this mess happened, and working with her full-time, but there was no way." I paused. This was the scary part, where I had to trust. "Now, if I... if I live with you, then I can quit the hospital, continue to work part-time with Dr. Metzger while I go to school."

Liam leaned forward, kissed me. Fiercely and with lots of tongue.

"That's a great idea, baby."

I was grinning and breathing hard and I looked to Porter to see what he thought.

"I love everything about it. And you."

"And since you're moving in, I am, too," Liam added, kissing me again and ending the conversation.

"We're in a hotel room in a snow storm. Nowhere to go. What should we do with ourselves?" Porter asked. "Talk?"

I could tell by the heated gleam in his eyes that talking was the last thing he wanted to do. I was all talked out. We'd worked through this mess, and it had been a big one, but we were together and better than ever. *This* was what love was all about. Unconditional, desperate.

It also helped that I was ridiculously attracted to both of them. I'd been shy at first, but no longer. Not when I'd thought I'd lost them. And Porter was right. We were all alone in the hotel, no one to bother us, no distractions and in a room with only a bed.

I tucked my fingers in the bottom of my sweatshirt, lifted it up an inch or two exposing my belly. "So I shouldn't take this off?"

IAM

THE NIGHT HAD GONE from hellish to heavenly. Here was our girl, sitting in my lap and lifting her sweatshirt over her head. Beneath, she had on a little tank top, one that hid nothing. White and threadbare, it molded to her lush tits and her nipples poked out.

As she lifted up to remove the garment, I gave her ass a light spank and she gasped. "Sass gets you spanked, baby."

Her eyes widened, then flared with heat. I spanked her again, the other ass cheek this time, then rubbed the heat in. Oh, our girl liked it.

"Liam," she said, her voice all breathy like a porn star. Our own sweet, sexy porn star. I wrapped an arm around her, angled her back and took a stiff peak into my mouth.

Her hands went to my head, tugged on my hair.

"Lucky she's got two men. A nipple for each of us," Porter said. "Wouldn't want one to be neglected."

I shifted her so she was angled his way, but never lifted my head. He joined me in pleasuring Jill. My fingers pushed up her little top and we lifted our heads long enough to get it off her. I never imagined I'd be into a threesome lifestyle, having my head right next to my best friend's working a woman's breasts, getting her off.

I'd thought I wasn't enough for Jill, that she wanted Porter, too, because I was... less. But it wasn't that at all. It took a huge cluster fuck for all of us to realize it wasn't Porter or me. Jill wanted Porter *and* me. We, all three of us, were a unit. Our own little family now. Someday, when Jill was ready, we'd have babies. Lots of them with her gorgeous eyes, sweet smile and feisty disposition.

She was happy and getting well-pleasured because she was with *both* her men. Jill was too much for just one man. She had so much love in her Porter and I were lucky enough to get it all.

And I'd spend the rest of my life showing her that.

"I want you naked. I want it all," she breathed.

Porter sat up, looked to me. Nodded.

Helping Jill to her feet in front of me, I slid her sweats down over her curvy hips, then turned my hand palm up to cup her pussy. She gasped as my fingers slid over her sopping folds.

"What do you want, sweetness?" Porter asked. He stood, began to shuck his clothes.

"Both of you," she said, her voice all breathy and erotic as fuck.

"You've got us, baby. We're not going anywhere."

"I want you to fuck me."

"Here?" I asked, curling two fingers so they slipped into

125

her. I slid a little deeper to find the spot she loved. I found the little textured spot and pressed.

"Yes!" she practically screamed.

I had to hope the hotel walls were soundproofed. Anyone walking by would know Jill was being well-satisfied by her men. And that thought made pre-cum spurt from my dick.

Her hand moved around behind her. While I couldn't see exactly what she was doing, when she said, "Here, too," I knew she was touching that virgin rosebud.

Porter stood watching, stroking his dick. "You take our girl, get her from all warmed up to burning hot. If Jill wants our dicks at the same time, cramming her pussy and ass nice and full, then I've got to go get some lube."

I nudged Jill in Porter's direction as I took a quick lick of her pussy juices from my fingers. Fuck!

"Where are you going?" Jill asked as Porter's hands roamed her body, as if he couldn't keep from touching her.

"I did a little shopping earlier. Got you a pretty new plug. They tossed small packets of lube in the bag. It's in my SUV."

"Hurry back," she said, standing there gloriously naked, her pussy all puffy and swollen from my finger play. Her nipples hard and damp from our mouths. Her cheeks all flushed. She was aroused and needy because of me and she stared at my dick. I could feel it snugly curved up toward my belt. "I want both my men."

Pre-cum seeped from me, eager to be in her. I grinned because I was heading out into the frigid cold. The sooner I got that lube, the sooner we got inside her. Got us together, made her ours... together, once and for all.

JILL

. . .

I HID a smile as Liam grabbed the key card and stormed from the room, but Porter quickly distracted me. He picked me up, settled me in the middle of the bed and lay down next to me. With his head propped up on his elbow, he looked me over. Every inch. His hand moved over me as he did so.

"How did I get so lucky?" he asked, although it seemed he was asking himself that question instead of me.

Goosebumps rose. "Cold?"

I shook my head. I was burning up. "You're teasing me."

A grin flashed on his face. "You think this is teasing?"

I squirmed as he palmed my breast, tugged on the nipple. "Yes!" I cried as my back arched.

He let go, moved so he was between my thighs. He was so big my legs were parted so wide. He scooped me up with his palms on my ass, my back lifting off the mattress and put his mouth on me.

"Porter!" I cried as he licked me from my weeping entrance and up to my clit. He gently licked along the top of one pussy lip to my clit and then down the other side.

By the time the door slammed shut behind Liam, I was writhing, whimpering. Begging.

Porter lifted his head and I couldn't miss how his mouth and chin were all wet. "All covered in honey," he said, then glanced at Liam who tossed little packets and a still-in-package butt plug onto the bed

His hands moved to unbutton his uniform shirt, the shoulders damp from snow. "Not fair."

"There's plenty for both of us."

Liam gave up on his shirt and moved Porter out of the way, taking over holding my hips. I looked down my body at him. His pale eyes met mine. "Let's get you ready for us to claim you together."

He didn't say more, just went at me—that's what he did, ravaged me with mouth, tongue and fingers—until it was too good, too much and I came, then came again. Sweat bloomed on my skin, my hair was a wild tangle I was sure, my voice scratchy from screaming. I was so blissed out that I missed the packet of lube being opened, but gasped as it was drizzled over my back entrance. I mewled at the contrast to how hot, wet and swollen my pussy was.

"Easy, baby. Just my finger for now. Got to get you all slick."

I felt a blunt finger brush over me there and I moaned. The sensations were so intense, especially since I'd already come. New nerve endings awakened and I was pushed back into full arousal all over again.

When he slipped a finger past my tightened ring, I whimpered, then groaned.

Soft suction surrounded a nipple. My eyes opened and saw Porter's head. I curled my fingers in his hair as he played. "That's what I like to hear, our girl's pleasure."

"I'm sure everyone on the floor heard," Liam commented as he slowly worked his finger deeper, then added more lube.

I couldn't even blush, for I didn't care. They'd know I was so damned happy.

One moment I was on my back, the next Porter was lying on the bed, feet touching the floor, and I was on top of him. When had he gotten undressed? His thick dick was pressed between our bellies.

My knees were on either side of his hips and I shifted, sliding my wet pussy up and down his length. He brushed my hair back and looked up at me. "Greedy for my dick, sweetness?"

I nodded and shifted so he settled right at my entrance. His hands dropped to his sides. "Have at it. Climb on and then Liam's going to get in on the action."

Gripping him at the base—he pulsed hot and thick in my hold—I lifted up onto my knees, then lowered myself until he slid in and I sank down all the way.

He growled. I groaned. I was so full and I leaned forward and kissed him, rolling my hips as I did. My clit rubbed against him and I clenched around him. I felt Liam's hand moving over my ass, cupping it, squeezing, before his thumb pressed against my slick back entrance. I cried out and clenched once more.

"Hurry… get… in… our… girl," Porter said between deep kisses. He widened his legs to make room for Liam.

As if he'd been waiting for the go ahead, Liam stepped close. His thumb moved away and was quickly replaced with the broad head of his cock. He must have slicked up because he slipped off and up toward my back.

Porter stilled me with a hand on my hip and Liam tried again.

"Relax, baby. Let me in, that's it. Good girl. Deep breath. Let it out. Yes! Shit, fuck, holy shit you're so tight."

I whimpered as the flared crown slipped past that tight ring of resistance.

"That's it, taking your men," Porter crooned. "So beautiful."

He kissed me, slowly, almost sweetly as Liam plundered my ass. Not hard, but insistent. Deep, then deeper still. My back arched and I couldn't believe how full I was. Two dicks. Both of them. In me.

Once Liam bottomed out, he stilled.

"I love you, baby. This is home. You between us…"

He didn't say more, couldn't. I couldn't see him well over

my shoulder, but I rested my head on Porter's chest, felt his heartbeat.

"Time to come, sweetness," Porter said, and began to move. Back, when Liam drove deep. They alternated. I couldn't move, couldn't do anything but feel.

Here, in this hotel room, cocooned not only by the snowstorm outside, but between the men I loved, I had everything.

And when I came, I cried out both their names. They soon followed. After cleaning up, I lay between them, safe. Protected. And definitely cherished.

NOTE FROM VANESSA

Don't worry, there's more Grade-A Beefcakes to come!

But guess what? I've got some bonus content for you with Jill, Porter and Liam. So sign up for my mailing list. There will be special bonus content for each Grade-A Beefcakes book, just for my subscribers. Signing up will let you hear about my next release as soon as it is out, too (and you get a free book…wow!)

As always…thanks for loving my books and the wild ride!

WANT MORE?

READ A SNEAK PEEK FROM SKIRT STEAK, BOOK FIVE IN THE GRADE-A BEEFCAKES SERIES.

It's Julia Duke's turn to find love… times two.

Remember: With a Vanessa Vale book, one cowboy is never enough. In this smokin' hot series, each heroine gets an extra helping (or two) of Grade-A Beefcake.

SKIRT STEAK

It wasn't even two minutes later when the doorbell rang. I looked at the clock on the microwave and realized it must be the strippers. They were early, but it didn't matter. Better than being late. When I opened the door, I froze. Gulped, hoped I didn't have drool on my chin. Holy hell, they were even hotter than the ones from the revue at Cassidy's.

Two, big, brawny guys stood before me. For age, I guessed early thirties. One was probably six foot, the other a few inches over. One dark, the other fair. The dark haired one—the guy on the right—had a close-cropped beard. Brown eyes. The blond's were fair. Their gazes roved over me from the top of my—most likely—wild red hair to my socked feet. They took their time in doing it, and I felt as if they didn't miss a single inch. Suddenly, I was hot all over and my nipples went hard.

If they were going to stare, then so was I. I catalogued the taut white t-shirt and leather jacket on Mr. Brown Eyes, the snug, long sleeved Henley on Blondie, the perfect fit of their well-worn jeans in *all* the right places. Oh, they definitely had what a stripper needed inside those pants. Rugged, virile, intense, dark. Even brooding. These two weren't cowboys. No snap shirts or Stetsons in sight.

"Hi, guys, you're here early," I said after clearing my throat. Suddenly, my mouth was very dry. Other parts of me... not so much, and I rubbed my thighs together.

"I'm Cash," Mr. Tall, Dark and Handsome said, tipping his head. "And this is Bennett." God, his voice was deep and... hot.

Colton

Ava was going to reconsider marrying my brother and Jed after getting a look at these two. A flare of jealousy made me pause and realize I was an idiot. They were *strippers* here for work. I wasn't the first woman who'd ogled them, and I wouldn't be the last.

"I'm Julia. I'm the one who arranged for you to come. I hope you like performing for bachelorette parties. All the ladies are due in about an hour for your little show, so you can hang out with me until then."

Bennett narrowed his eyes and studied me again, making me *very* self-conscious. They weren't trying to date me, just work a job. I exhaled, realizing I was being ridiculous. "Little show?" he asked.

I bit my lip and understood I'd pricked his vanity. How, I wasn't exactly sure because there was no way women weren't tossing their panties at them wherever they went. Even fully clothed. Their self-confidence must be through the roof.

"Yeah, sorry about that." I glanced down at my green socks, then back at them. "I didn't mean to make light of your job. Entertaining horny women can't be easy, especially when you're practically naked. I couldn't be a stripper."

They glanced down at my body, as if assessing me for the role.

"Why not? You've got the body," Bennett replied.

I gave a little huff of a laugh. I wasn't supermodel skinny, nor had centerfold boobs like Ava, and I had fiery red hair that had a mind of its own. "I've got no moves." *No moves at all, per Frank.*

I stepped back so they could come in.

"You mentioned entertaining horny women. Are *you* horny?" Cash asked, taking a step toward me, making me tip my chin up to meet his eyes. Instantly, I wondered how that beard would feel against my inner thighs. *Down, girl!*

He was just flirting, a professional stripper. Flirting was part of the job. It definitely brought in more tips. But that was all it was. Sexy banter. They weren't serious about me.

"What woman wouldn't be, looking at you two?" I responded, tilting my head to see Bennett, too.

A slow grin spread across Bennett's face. "I'm not interested in all women, just you."

Oh. If looks could kill, I'd be dead... from orgasms. And my panties were definitely ruined now.

"Well, um... sure. Guys aren't the only ones who think about sex all the time. Good thing I've got dildos for party favors. It's like the real thing, without all the complaints. Come on, you can help me finish with the bags."

They didn't say anything, just stared at me wide-eyed, then looked at each other for a moment.

"Do you have costumes or props or anything you need to bring in?" I tried to look past them and out the door, but they were so big they blocked the view of the street.

"No," Cash said.

I nodded once. "Right. You're probably already wearing those little banana hammocks. That little scrap of stretchy fabric is all the costume you need, right?" Pointing toward the front of their jeans, I circled my finger about.

When they stared at me as if I sprouted a second head, I thought about what I'd said. "God, sorry." I put my hand over my eyes for a moment in shame, shook my head. "Not *little*. I mean, sure, a G-string isn't all that much material, but I'm sure you're both *very* big. I didn't mean to insult you... um, there."

Cash grinned and I realized I sounded like a lunatic. No wonder I didn't have a boyfriend. "Right, I'll shut up now. Come on in."

I heard the door close and they followed me through Kaitlyn's house to the kitchen.

When I looked over my shoulder at them, I caught Tall, Dark and Handsome checking out my ass.

I blushed and stood in front of the favor bags again, not exactly sure how to entertain them. "I, um, just need to finish these up." I reached into the box and pulled out two dildos. "Here." I handed one to each of them. When Blondie's eyebrows went up practically under his hair, I laughed. "Each bag gets a dildo and the other favors. They're all lined up there." I pointed to the other side of the table. "One in each."

They studied the dildos in their hands. "Why do you need one of these? I'm sure your boyfriend knows what he's doing," Cash said.

I grabbed a bag and went around to the other favor items. I dropped a little lavender scented soap into the bag, then a bath bomb. "No boyfriend," I replied.

"You said something about complaints. If you don't like using a dildo, there are other toys."

I looked up at Bennett's comment, then grabbed a steamy paperback from the pile, dropped it in the bag. I thought of Frank, of what he'd said to me. The asshole. "The dildo's great," I finally answered. "It doesn't complain when it's fucking me."

I bit my lip, realized I said too much and put the bag down. Strippers or not, they were strangers, and they didn't need to know this stuff. Taking a deep breath, I pasted on a smile. "I never offered you a drink. Can I get you something?"

They were staring at me. Again. Still. This time, their eyes were narrowed, jaws clenched. Bennett still held the neon green dildo and was practically strangling it.

"Who complains when fucking you? What's his name?" he asked.

The front door slammed shut before I could say more. "Hello!"

Ava. *Thank god.*

"In here," I called and the men put the dildos on the table. Ava breezed in, all smiles and perfect, Miss America hair. I hated that she looked so good all the time. I'd never seen her without at least mascara and lip gloss. She lived on a ranch in Montana, not Park Avenue, and I wanted to hate her for being so flipping perfect. But, I couldn't.

With her in the room, I looked like a hot mess. My red hair was wild and always unruly. I didn't have on any makeup, and I was in a t-shirt and jeans.

"Guys, this is Ava—"

"Bennett!" Ava said, giving him a hug as if they knew each other. "Cash, it's been a while," she added when she turned to Mr. Dark and Deadly.

I frowned. *What the hell?*

The intense looks they'd been giving me fell away and they smiled at Ava.

"Any more problems with that four wheeler?" Cash asked her.

She shook her head, her styled curls sliding across her shoulders. "Nope, the new carburetor did the trick."

Carburetor? Since when did she know about engine parts? She ran the Seed and Feed, but still. And why was she asking these two? I posed the obvious question. "You guys know each other?"

Ava stepped out of Bennett's hug, but put her hand on his arm. "Of course. Cash owns the auto shop on Main. He's the one who towed your truck this morning."

My mouth fell open as I looked to him. He grinned at me and winked.

I'd been helping Gus, Kemp and Poe with a company web site and, when done, I went out to my truck parked in front of their office to discover it wouldn't start. Kemp had given me a ride here to Kaitlyn's and said he'd take care of getting it to the mechanic. I just didn't know it had been Cash.

"And Bennett's building that custom bike for Jed I told you about." *Colton*

Towed trucks… Custom bike… Carburetors…

"I thought… I thought—" I sputtered, looked at the men. Holy shit. Yeah, they knew *exactly* what I thought.

Bennett ran a hand over the back of his neck and offered me a wicked smile.

These two hotties weren't strippers at all.

Read Skirt Steak now!

ABOUT THE AUTHOR

Vanessa Vale is the *USA Today* Bestselling author of over 50 books, sexy romance novels, including her popular Bridgewater historical romance series and hot contemporary romances featuring unapologetic bad boys who don't just fall in love, they fall hard. When she's not writing, Vanessa savors the insanity of raising two boys and figuring out how many meals she can make with a pressure cooker. While she's not as skilled at social media as her kids, she loves to interact with readers.

www.vanessavaleauthor.com
facebook.com/vanessavaleauthor
instagram.com/vanessa_vale_author

28198224R00086

Made in the USA
San Bernardino, CA
06 March 2019